TOTALI

Compilation of nine
talks delivered by Miss
Vimala Thakar and one
question-answer session
conducted by her in
Ceylon between 24th
February and 11th
March 1971.

TOTALITY IN ESSENCE

Vimala Thakar

MOTILAL BANARSIDASS PUBLISHERS
PRIVATE LIMITED ● DELHI

First Edition: Delhi, 1971
Reprint: Delhi, 1986, 1995, 2002

© VIMAL PRAKASHAN TRUST, AHMEDABAD

ISBN: 81-208-0048-6

Also available at:

MOTILAL BANARSIDASS
41 U.A. Bungalow Road, Jawahar Nagar, Delhi 110 007
236, 9th Main III Block, Jayanagar, Bangalore 560 011
8 Mahalaxmi Chamber, Bhulabhai Desai Rd., Mumbai 400 026
120 Royapettah High Road, Mylapore, Chennai 600 004
Sanas Plaza, 1302 Baji Rao Road, Pune 411 002
8 Camac Street, Kolkata 700 017
Ashok Rajpath, Patna 800 004
Chowk, Varanasi 221 001

Printed in India
BY JAINENDRA PRAKASH JAIN AT SHRI JAINENDRA PRESS,
A-45 NARAINA, PHASE-I, NEW DELHI 110 028
AND PUBLISHED BY NARENDRA PRAKASH JAIN FOR
MOTILAL BANARSIDASS PUBLISHERS PRIVATE LIMITED,
BUNGALOW ROAD, DELHI 110 007

CONTENTS

: 1 :
(**24th February, 1971**)

Friends, I deem it a privilege and an honour to be amongst you this evening. This is my first visit to your land and I am as much surprised as you might be that a person who is not known in any of the political, economic, social or religious fields of Indian life has been invited by a few individuals to come and speak here in Ceylon.

Life has very strange ways of bringing people together. And I come here in all humility to share with you my concern about the fundamental problems with which humanity the world over is confronted today. Not as a Guru, teacher or preacher bringing you some message, I could not do that. I do not represent any particular religion, any particular organisation, institution. Nor do I represent any individual, living or dead. I have no claims to any authority, spiritual or worldly, not even of erudition or scholarship. Nor have I any claims to interpret Hindu religion, Hindu philosophy, or any other teachings of any individual. Being one of you, the billions that are inhabiting the globe, one does feel concerned about the situation which is prevalent in the world.

As you know, I come from the land which is stormed to-day by restlessness in all fields of life—political, economic, cultural, educational, religious, moral and so on. While wandering across the countries, travelling through East and West, it seems to me that a huge storm, a ferocious storm of restlessness, rebelliousness, is breaking upon the shores of human psyche. Whether you are in Japan or you are in U.S.A., you may be in the West European countries, or you may be visiting the East European countries, you may be in the Middle East, you find the human consciousness being visited by a very great storm. That restlessness, the revolt that is raging furiously, not only among the young people, the desire to break down everything that is established, the values, the norms, the criteria, the standards, the political theories, the economic theories and so on, is enormous. And I feel very glad that this has happened.

The age-old and worn out theories and values are cracking, the temples, the churches, the mosques are tumbling down. It is a very great challenge to the constructive genius of the youth, because human beings cannot live in psychological vacuum. So this is a challenge to my generation. The constructive and creative genius of the young people the world over has to find out what the foundation of life is going to be to-morrow. What is going to be the way of living ? And that is why I feel that the challenge of a total revolution is the basic challenge, whether you are in the starving East or you are in the countries suffering from affluence. The cultural poverty of affluence is as glaring as the cultural poverty of starvation-stricken countries.

So, as one of the human beings, not standing on a pedestal of religion or spirituality, but as a living sensitive human being, feeling concerned, I come here to share with you through words, as far as words can carry us, the observations and the understanding that has happened to visit me and passed through me. I do not think understandings of truth can be monopolised by individuals or institutions. They are events in the evolution of human consciousness. So, whether it is liberation, enlightenment, or illumination, they cannot become vested interest of individuals, sects, communities, countries or states. They are just simple events.

Now what do I imply by the term 'total revolution' and why do I use the adjective 'total' ? The world has known revolutions and people interested in revolutions dividing life either as the individual and the social or collective, or, the inner and the outer. Those who felt concerned about an inner revolution, revolution in the psyche, revolution in the consciousness, did not worry so much about the texture and quality of collective relationships. And efforts have been made in the East in that direction. A seeker of truth, a seeker of better life, retiring from the responsibility of the so-called daily life, retiring in search of truth, liberation and God, has been one way.

In the West, on the other hand, man felt concerned with the

search outside the skin, discovering the nature of the five elements, finding out ways and means of conquering them. That is how science and technology grew in the West to astounding dimensions. It was the concern of the occident to change the outer patterns of life, the social structure, the economic pattern, the monetary structure, the political set-ups, the set-ups of administration etc. Thus the occidentals concerned themselves with changing the outer patterns of life, not paying much attention to and not feeling much concern about the quality of individual behaviour and the quality of individual consciousness.

There have been two ways of approaching the problem of change that is necessary. It goes without saying that the conditions in which man is living to-day are simply unbearable. Man knows how to fly in the air like the birds. He knows how to swim in the water like the fish. As Bertrand Russel has put it long ago, he does not yet know how to live on earth like a human being in love, in peace, in harmony ; in love and peace and harmony with himself, with his body, with his mind—with the totality of his being. He does not also know how to live spontaneously. The elegance of spontaneity, the beauty of humility and innocence is something we hardly come across. In collective relationships we miss the atmosphere of love, friendihip and peace. We may talk in the name of peace and love ; all the religions the world over are doing that. But man has not yet become mature enough to live in harmony and friendship with other fellow human beings collectively. So, this is the real challenge.

I know there are problems of starvation and poverty in Asia and Africa and unless the starvation is eliminated, you cannot talk about re ligion and spirituality in those continents. The primary concern is to bring the human beings from the sub-human to a decent human level. There is the problem of violence. But the political and economic problems appear to me to be symptoms of a deeper malady. They are the symptoms of a deeper malady rooted in the human consciousness aud unless one tackles the roots of the malady in the individual, not in isolation, not in retirement from life, but actually in the battle-field of daily life, unless one tackles the roots there, unless one finds out a way of growing out of the overpowering animal tendencies and drives and blind passion in daily behaviour, the symptoms cannot be eliminated by themselves. Do what you will. They cannot be eliminated by indoctrinating people into new thoughts, into new ways of reacting.

Organisation of human thoughts, systematisation of human feelings and emotions, standardisation and regimentation of thoughts and feelings has been indulged in for bygone centuries. We will go into that issue later on in this talk. But feeding the human brain with new patterns of physical and psychological behaviour does not seem to have helped humanity much in eliminating exploitation, violence, brutality, callousness, etc.

So, those who really feel seriously interested in this crisis in the human psyche will have to sit down quietly and think about the whole issue with great concern. The difficulty is from where to get that sustained seriousness which will enable us to look into the issue without any preference or prejudice, intellectual or emotional. Sustained seriousness is a very difficult thing and we are used to live on the superficial layer of consciousness. When we come across the problem that stimulates the emotions, we get disturbed for a few minutes and then the momentum of the stimulation subsides, and so does the mental disturbance subside too, and then we go back to the daily routine. You hear on the radio, if you are in Europe and America you see on the television, the bloodshed, the murders and you say, "ah! how ghastly! how beastly! that's terrible!" and so on, a few exclamations for five or ten minutes, the whole thing goes down, subsides, and then talks about icecreams, cinemas and parties come back.

Emotional disturbance leading to a nervous tension is not sustained seriousness. Or, one gets intellectually disturbed. The pet theories, the conclusions, the ideologies that one has cherished through one's whole life are realised to be unsuitable and incapable of solving the problems and one feels restless and gets disturbed. That intellectual disturbance may not result in sustained seriousness which is a state of one's whole being, in which there is humility, there is receptivity. In that state one is able to brush aside the preferences and prejudices, the likes and dislikes, the opinions and evaluations that one has cherished and nourished, not condemn them, not brush them aside in a derogatory sense, not throw them away, but for the sake of a real enquiry one brushes them aside and says to oneself, - "by jove, I do not know, it has not helped me uptil now. What will happen if I look at the problems from a different angle altogether ? Let me enquire." Sustained seriousness leads to a genuine enquiry born in the heart. It is not an intellectual curiosity to be gratified by new theories and new ways of behaviour. It is not an emotional disturbance which can be gratified by finding out consolation and support and shelter in a powerful individual, whether he has the power of money, whether he has the power of technology, science, or the occult world. It is not concerned with finding out consolation, shelter and refuge.

Enquiry needs the austerity of humility and sustained seriousness always leads to the awakening of a genuine enquiry. Let us find out for ourselves—can there be a way out ? So it seems to me that for finding out what a total revolution will be, one will have to brush aside age-old theories and notions. Life has neither inside nor outside. Inside the skin and outside the skin are categories created by the human mind because of the limitations of the sense-organs. Life is neither visible nor invisible, neither tangible nor intangible. The tangibility and intangibility, the visibility and the invisibility are reflections upon the limitations of human sense-organs. They are not descriptions of reality.

Life is neither individual nor collective. Life is one indivisible whole, Unity is the nature of life. So we will have to brush-aside the age-old dichotomies that we have cherished, and get rid of the curse of fragmentation that has been upon the human mind, of dividing life into individual and collective, the inner and the outher, the physical and the psychological. Life is one indivisible whole. It cannot be fragmented. That is the beauty of life. You cannot divide life and say that this is true for the physiological, and untrue for the psychological. There cannot be one set of values for the physical and physiological, and another set of values for the psychological, one set of values for the individual

life another set of values for the family life, and a third set of
values, for the social and economic life,

Man has divided life, He has created various codes of
conduct and sets of values and patterns of behaviour and these
are inconsistent and sometimes contradictory to one another and
man carries in himself all these contradictory values and inconsistent patterns of behaviuur and he wants to play different roles,
the role of an individual, the role of a family man, the role of a
political leader, the role of an economic organiser, the role of
an educationist and so on. And carrying all the inconsistent
patterns, opposing trends of behaviour, contradictory sets of values,
man has become neurotic, He is a split personality. He tries
to balance the contradictory and mutually incompatible patterns
of behaviour and he uses hypocrisy, suppression. denial and
arrogance as his shields while carrying the contradictions and
incompatibles within himself, Trying to live upto these various
sets of behaviour he gets tremendous pressure on his nervous
system and no wonder that man the world over lives in a neurotic
state. I do hope that the implications of the expression 'neurotic
state' would not be misinterpreted. When I cannot look at a
thing, when I cannot look at an individual; or a challenge without
a nervous tension and a chemical pressure in the body, I am
neurotic. How to look at a thing, to look at an individual in a
relaxed way, not having a nervous tension or a chemical pressure
in the body ?

The perception in total relaxation results in responses which
are spontaneous, which leave no soars and scratches. So, I do feel
that the way we are living to-day,—I am not referring to the
people in Ceylon; I am not referring onlv to the people in India,
but I am referring to man with capital 'M' throughout the world,—
we are living in a neurotic way. When I get angry, what happens
to me ? I get angry and that leads to certain tensions and preessures
in me—the heat generated in my body, the tension on the optical
and auditory nerves, the contraction that I feel in the bowels,
in my digestive process. The tensions and pressures oblige me
and compel me to behave in a certain way, The words that
escape the mouth of an angry man, the gestures, the glance that

escapes his eyes—what are they ? What quality do they have ? Don't they have the quality of imbalancc ? Don't they have the quality of crudeness, cruelty ? So, if I get angry half-a-dozen times a day am I not going through momentary imbalance or insanity, momentary attacks of neurosis ? If I feel envious, what happens to me ? When I want to dominate over another individual, what is going on within me ? Every day we go through the desire to dominate, to own and we go through the feeling of jealousy, ambition, and its tension, anger and its pressures. That is the stuff of our life. And daily life is the only life that we have, not what we do in the temples and the mosques for an hour or two.

What I do for the twenty-four hours of the day is the real substance of my life and the odour that that substance has, cannot be hidden from the world. I give to the world what I am. So, when I say that man is living in a neurotic state to-day, it is a question of difference of degree, and this is unbearable. Whether I have a gun or a revolver in my hand in that state of imbalance; or, I have a spear, or a sword, or an arrow and bow in my hands, is immaterial, But if the savage in me persists, if the animal instinct of fear persists in me, and creates its own inhibitions and gets reflected in my relationship with others, then I think, I am a factor contributing to the violence, the aggression that exists in the world, That is how violence is born, that is how the wars are created. First, we have them in our hearts, the daily share of violence that we have in ourselves, the aggression, the injustice, the exploitation,—emotional, intellectual, economic, that we go through, we Indulge in, Thus the seeds of world wars are sown in individual human hearts.

The tension that humanity is going through. can be experienced in my behaviour with you and your behaviour with me, That is why I say that individuals are the real centres of total revolution. Individuals will have to a-k themselves—can man behave in a different way ? — Not a neurotic way, Can man grow into a different dimension of consciousness from which he can behave in total relaxation, from where he can use his brain accurately, precisely, mathematically, and yet in innocence in humility ? Is it possible for him to use the body and the mind with the elegance of innocence and beauty of humility ? Or, is man doomed to live a prisoner of the instincts, thoughts, feelings and conditioned reflexes ? Or, is it possible to grow out of this into an entirely new dimension of consciousness ? It seems to me, it is possible.

Man is not using his total brain to-day, Man is using only a fraction, Even the physical brain is not totally tapped and explored. There are untapped and unexplored parts in the human brain, So. there is a dimension to human consciousness which is not yet explored by man, What will happen if man grows into that dimension ? Then the dimension of love and friendsihp might become the way of his living, That is why I appeal to individuals. Man has to become mature. Wherever we are, the quest, the problem, the challenge is to transform the texture or quality of human relationships. So how to convert the human relationships into occasions for self-discovery, and how to convert those relationships into occasions for self-transformation ? The transformation that needs isolation, withdrawal from life, running away from the responsibilities of life has no value for me. That may lead to the attainment of occult and transcendental powers; just as the East has been drunk with the power of the occult and transcendental for thousands of years, You may visit India, its various parts; you come across *Yogis*, and *Sanyasis* and those who can awaken the *Kundalini*, those who can show you the miracles of the occult and the transcendental. But look at the people, my brothers and sisters in India, and the state of their life in the villages as well as the towns. Personal achievements and the transcendental, arrived at in isolation from daily responsibility, have no value as far as the human problems are concernd.

The challenge is of a total revolution which will work in the individual and the collective simultaneously, which will work in the inside as well as the outside simultaneously and the revolution that will take place, exactly where we are, in the midst of people, in the midst of human relationship. That is whyI call it a total revolution, not a partial, not a fragmentary one. I would not like to divide and fragment it.

We have not got any precedent in history for such a total revolution. It cannot be called spiritual, it cannot be called individual. All these labels put together, perhaps might give an honest description of what I mean by the totality of life. Uptil now, there is no precedent because religions, spirituality, discovery of truth, have been looked upon as something aloof and independent of our daily life, our physical, our mental, our intellectual life. The consciousness will have to be purged of the illusion that there is a division in life like secular, mundane, spiritual and religious.

Religion for me is personal discovery of truth. It is a personal discovery of the meaning of life. The meaning of life cannot be borrowed. It cannot be emotionally imposed upon me. It cannot be intellectually indocrinated into me. Intellectual acquisition of theories, of ideologies and ideas, is not understanding of the truth. Intellectual acquisition, what we call knowledge, has not got the dynamism to result in personal discovery of truth. Knowledge is sterile. The intellect acquires information. You store it in memory. You put it under different categories You give it labels and names. Then with the help of ethics and morality, you provide certain incentives to the individual to behave upto the knowledge that he has acquired. If knowledge had dynamism to get translated instantaneously into action, man would not need incentives in the name of ethics, religion or spirituality. So knowledge has no dynamism of its own, It is only a cerebral activity of receiving information, retaining it in memory, invoking it again when needed. It is a mechanical activity and the computers and electronic brains and the way they worked, have proved it beyond doubt that cerebral activity is a mechanistic activity. It has no originality, it has no creativity. It is a constructive activity, not creative.

Thus personal discovery of truth cannot be a cerebral activity. It cannot be an intellectual activity. And the essence of religion is personal discovery of the meaning of life, personal discovery of the totality of life. The religious person is he who lives in the awareness of the unity of life. The religious person is he who lives in the burning awareness of that totality. Whatever he does physically, mentally, verbally, is done in the light of the unity of life. The total revolution that is needed today could not be given a label as religious or spiritual, and it has no precedent in history, Those who feel seriously concerned today will have to break a new path, We cannot look upto someone, We have no blue-prints, And we have no one to guide us, There is a challenge to the creative genius of the younger generation, They have no authority to depend upon, no guide to give a helping hand.

A guided enquiry can lead to reform, which is modified continuity. Here we have no guidance and no Masiah, no teacher, no master. So the enquiry has to be conducted with a sense of responsibility that freedom brings with it. It is not easy to live in freedom· Freedom is a fire that can consume you unless you have a sense of responsibility to use it properly· So, without any guidance and authority we have to conduct the enquiry in the light of the flame of freedom· Those who have no paths, no blueprints will have to have the pliability of a scientist, of a research scholar, who has a kind of tentative approach. We cannot afford to indulge in any dogmatism whatsoever at any stage of our enquiry· We are going to find out what a total revolution is. Dogmatism is asserting that what one has perceived is the total truth, and that is the only truth. Dogmas are born this way. The discovery of truth needs the humility which will give pliability to the mind, a kind of tentativity that the scientific researcher needs to bring his scientific approach to human life· Thus alongwith courage and fearlessness, we will need the tentativity, the pliability of approach. It is very difficult to observe what is discovered without allowing it to be coloured by one's conditionings, without imposing one's subjective reaction on the little discovery that one has made. That is why I refer to the sustained seriousness, which is absolutely necessary for an enquiry to be born in the heart.

For the last fifty minutes what we have done is to unroll the canvas on which further meetings in Ceylon would be conducted. The first point that I made was — I come here to share and not to teach or preach simply because I don't feel I am equal to the task of teaching or preaching anything, I feel it below self-respect to cast a shadow on the face of any fellow human being. The sensitivity of love does not allow me to assert or preach. I don't want to convince anyone, to convert anyone. Sharing in friendship is something very beautiful, You sit on the footing of equality and you share. If I have the motive to convince you, to convert you, to propound, to propagate, {then it will be a very subtle kind of violence committed against you. This is a new relationship between listeners and speakers,

This verbal communication for the joy of sharing in love and frienship, is something new, a new dimension in public meetings or group meetings; and I hope that what I say will be believed, though it may sound unbelievable. This is so new, especially for a person who is called spiritual or religious. I don't know even if I could be called a spiritual person at all from any angle, from any approach. I am a person who loves life tremendously. I am passionately in love with life and nothing has diverted my attentin from living. I am passionately in love with man and nothing can divert my attention from friendship with man, So the verbal communication that will take place between us should be on this level.

The second point was that humanity is passing through a crisis. Individually man is becoming more and more neurotic, collectively more and more tense, The whole world is in revolt and the huge storm of restlessness and revolt is breaking upon the shores of human payche. This is the challenge. We may try to turn away our gaze from the restlessness and from the revolt, but life won't allow us to do it very long. We will have to open our eyes and ears,

We proceeded to the implications of the word 'total', how life is one and indivisible and how revolutions cannot be fragmented. The problems that appear to be in the political, the economic, the cultural and the other collective flelds are only symptoms of a deeper malady and the malady is—man has lost the elegance of innocence, spontaneity and relaxation while he was busy sophisticating his brain. He was busy sophisticating the patterns of physiological and psychological behaviour and he missed this. So he became one sided and had lop-sided growth and to-day he has to live under nervous tensions and chemical pressures throughout the day and perhaps also through the night. And a person who is under nervous tension and chemical pressure, who cannot live spontaneously and cannot behave in a relaxed way, how can he create a society where there is no injustice, aggression, violence and, therefore, no war ? How can he create a society where there is no exploitation and, therefore, no classes ? Wiping out the state boundaries, creating societies without eliminating exploitation, the dreams that were seen in the 19th century by the great noble visionary Marx, as well as by Gandhi in India, why have they not come true to-day in spite of efforts by thousands in the East and West ? This is a very serious question. So we proceed to say that revolutions cnnnot be fragmented.

Revolutions will have to be total and the beginning will have to be made in individnal life. Initiative will have to be taken by the individual who will be a living centre of new revolution, But he will be a centre of revolution only when he does not run away from his daily life in the name of religion and spirituality, when he faces the challenge of transforming the quality of his behaviour.

How the revolution cannot be a cerebral activity, how man can go beyond the frontiers of his own brain, without using it, will be taken up in the next meeting.

Talks are the flowers that blossom in the soil of communion that takes place between the listener and the speaker, The speaker cannot claim the talk for himself or herself. The participation of the listener is as important as the elocution of the speaker. So I would like to thank each one of you who has been kind enough to come here and listen to me. Secondly, I would like to thank those courageous persons who dared invite me here. They had not met me, they had not seen me, they had not known me, they had not heard me. I appreciate their courage, admire their courage, in not only inviting but arranging so many meetings for me. So, with this expression of gratitude for all the members of the Reception Committee and expression of· gratitude for all the listners, I beg to take your leave now.

: 2 :

(26th Februa y, 1971)

As I had observed the other day in the public meeting, the basic challenge to-day is Psychic Revolution—a transformation in the consciousness of human beings. Consciousness is not the speciality of the human race. The mineral world, the plant world and the animal world have also a kind of consciousness. Animals can sing. They can feel. They can react. They have a kind of sensitivity. One may call the animal consciousness, simple consciousness of receiving a sensation and reacting to it. But the human being has emerged with a new quality of self-consciousness. Man is capable of knowing a thing and simultaneously of being aware that he knows it. He is capable of doing a thing and simultaneously of being aware that he is doing it, not only that he is doing it, but even why he is doing it.

To do a thing, to be aware of the action, the process of action and also to be aware of the motivation forces working behind it. It is due to this capacity of self-consciousness that man could develop the culture and civilization that he has developed in bygone centuries. It is due to this self consciousness that man could coin words as symbols for communication.

Semantics and linguistics would not have been possible if man did not know what was happening inside him and did not have the urge to communicate the inner happenings to his fellow human beings. The inter-action between the outer and the inner being is shared by man with his fellow human beings. It is this capacity of self-consciousness which enabled man to develop the social sciences as well as natural sciences. He is capable of conceptualisation. Conceptualization is to go through an experience, to deduce certain conclusions from that concrete experience and formulate a concept or an idea. If man were not capable of ideation or conceptualisation, sciences like Physics, Chemistry and all the advance in science and technology would not have been possible.

We must know that we use concepts and symbols based on those concepts for our verbal communication.

I wonder if you have noticed that the mathematical figures, the numbers and their mutual relationship was arbitrarily decided by man, thousands of years ago. He has been using the arithmetical figures for all feats of engineering. He had the concept of a point without magnitnde, without length and on the supposition of that point are based all the sciences like geometry, trignometry, and arts like sculpture and architecture. So also man developed the concept of time which includes space.

Time, as we use it, is a concept and not a fact. The relationship between the revolutions of the earth and the Sun is a relative fact. We have cut reality into small pieces. Sixty seconds constituting a minute have no reality of their own. They have conceptual reality and relative utility for communication. But we mistake concepts and symbols for facts, even for reality. One has to see this very clearly that time as we use it, has no reality of its own. Really speaking, there is no division, thare is no fragmentation. Life only exists in its pure isness. Just as you use money,— the rupee, the dollar, the sterling, as a currency, similarly, the currency of psychological time has been used. You have a monetary structure for your economic order in society and in the same way you have the time structure for order in collective relationship. This use of time as a concept has led man to imagine yesterdays and to-morrows.

There is no yesterday and there is no to-morrow. Life only 'is'. The concept of to-morrow provokes fear. The concept of yesterday stimulates memory. We live either in the memory of the past or in the fear of future. The inhibitions of fear and indulgence in memory consume most of the time. We have no time to live in the present. We have no time to live in the Now, in the Moment. A direct, immediate relationship with the isness of life is missed.

I wonder if yon have ever noticed that the concept of ego, of 'I' consciousness is also a symbol. We use the word 'I' and 'mine', 'the me' and the 'not me', the 'I' and 'the other', hundred times a day. Do we ever ask ourselves what this 'I' is ? It is the name given by parents to a child to discriminate the child from other children. The attributes of the body of the child are described by the parents, and by the neighbours. They say, the child is beautiful or it is ugly. The child comes to believe that it is ugly or beautiful. Then there are the attributes of the mind and the brain. The attributes of the body and the mind, the judgements of the people, the opinions and evaluations of society becom layers of identification. They get crystallised in the consciousness.

Thus the 'I' consciousness with which the child grows, is again the result of concepts and symbols that man has evolved. The identiflcation with all these associations goes so deep into the child that he really believes that the limitations of the body and the mind are his own limitations. Instead of getting acquainted with the physical and the psychological organism, instead of discovering what he is, he grows with the conviction that he is the physical and the psychological structure.

Thus we live in concepts. We live in symbols; we have no intimate and direct touch with the reality. That is our life. Ideas are always about facts. Concepts are always about facts. They have been developed by man collectively through centuries. What we call our thoughts, feelings, sentiments, emotions, and our reflexes, voluntary or involuntary, really do not belong to us.

There is nothing like an individual mind. There is the Hindu mind, the Muslim mind, the Catholic mind, the Protestant mind, the Buddhist mind, the Zen mind or the Communist nind. And now, among the Communists, the Marxist mind, the Maoist mind and so on. It is something collective, fed into the individual brain. Thoughts, feelings, emotions are all patterns of behaviour based on concepts and symbols fed systematically into the human brain, which is a very sensitive, very sophisticated, very complex and very rich instrument. It is a beautiful instrument. But one has to understand the mechanism of mind, the whole chemistry of thought and emotion, before one can talk of religion or spirituality.

Religion which is a personal discovery of truth can never take place until I know what I am. It is the ignorance about oneself, about the mechanism of mind, that causes half the misery in the world. One who is ignorant about the mechanism of mind cannot use it properly. We do not know how to handle our minds. It is ignorance of the known that creates the fear of the unknown. It is the ignorance of the bondage that creates the illusion of freedom. So one has to come to grips with what we look upon as the known. The known must be re-discovered. It must not remain merely as the known. The discovery and the understanding will enable us to penetrate through the known.

Thus we have to see that mind is the product of collective human society. We carry within our consciousness all the knowledge and experience of the human race, right from the first human animal who must have inhabited the globe, upto the sophisticated cerebral activity of the twentieth century man.

You have seven basic notes in music, and you can play with them and you can create different melodies with their help. In the same way, you can use words, 'the basic concept', and write poetry. You can write novels. You take the point, the line, the circle, the triangle, the square and you can play upon them, by permutation and combination. Thus we can indulge in a variety of constructive activities based on these concepts. But that is not creation. It is only a constructive activity.

So one has to realise that the anger that comes up in one is not one's anger, but is a pattern of behaviour fed into the self. One has to realise that the sensitivity to acquire information, which is called intellectual brilliance, is not a personal attribute or quality but a tendency fed into the brain. One has to realise that no thought and no emotion belongs to any one personally. It is a momentum working on its own, in human life stored into the sub-conscious and the unconscious. There is very little that man consciously acquires. The conscious mind or the uppermost layer of consciousness contains the purposeful, intentional acquisition of knowledge and experience. But the rest of it is a biological and psychological inheritance.

So when a sense organ comes into contact with an object and receives an impression, and when that impression stimulates an electromagnetic impulse in the body, which is carried by the nervous system to the brain and the brain reacts, it is a mechanistic activity. It is not a creative movement. Thinking, feeling and willing are all mechanistic. This fact disturbs the human being. All the vanity and pride of one's opinions, conclusions, evaluations and the order of priorities tumbles down. It collapses the moment one realises that mental activity is mechanistic. And it is high time that man realises this simple fact.

In the West, man has to co-exist with the computer. The computers taking over the whole statistical department of U.S.A. is a very serious challenge to the thinking, sensitive person. The computers function with more precision and accuracy than the human mind. The human perception gets twisted by chemical pressure of emotion at the moment of perception. But the computer's perception is precise. It does not get twisted or distorted. When we look at a thing, it is our emotion that looks. If we are angry, disturbed, or jealous, the instrument of perception gets distorted whenever the mind is disturbed. The chemical disturbance at any given moment, distorts the act of perception or audition. It naturally inhibits the response. Computers do not suffer from this malady of chemical disturbance.

Thus the co-existence of computer and human being poses a very serious challenge, and man is eager to find out what is more to the human consciousness than reception and retention of information in memory and re-invocation of the same. To go beyond mind is no more a Utopian question. It is not a mere religious or spiritual question. It is one of the most serious challenges for us.

I would like to point out with all humility that the moment spent in repetitive activity is not lived. The time spent in mechanistic, repetitive activity is not lived because it is not the person but the habit that reacts to the situation. It is the habit-pattern that reacts. It is worth observing how much time of the day is spent in reacting according to the habit structure. The relationship between husband and wife, relationship with children, with neigh-

bours, has perhaps become a pattern of living. It has lost its dynamism. If you so observe, you will notice as I have done that most
of the time is spent in reacting according to the conditionings.
Even our getting angry, being aggressive, is done out of instincts.
One is not fully aware of what is happening and of what one is
doing.

To live is to be aware of the minutest movement taking place
'within me' in relation to the 'without me',—to be aware of the
total movement of life, within the skin and outside the skin, the
minutest movement of the body, of the mind, the objective challenge, the subjective reaction and their chemical impact upon the
organism. The moments spent in awareness are lived and the
moments spents in repeating habits and conditioning patterns, are
not lived. This is the difference between living and vegetating. Living involves total action, which involves spontaneity and awareness, and hence is qualitatively different from repetitive, mechanical action. Animals also respond and react according to the instincts fed into their organism. What is the difference between insti-
nctual repetition and repetition out of discrimination, out of knowledge, out of morality, out of religious concepts and out of political ideas ? They are all stored, crystallised and man goes on mechanically reacting according to them.

As long as one is living according to something stored in memory one is living in the past and not in the present. To live, on
the other hand, is to be with the beauty of the present moment; to
be with the now, the here, the present, It seems that mind and brain do not help us to live with the present, with the now or with
the here.

Another aspect of mental activity is worth noticing. It is an
indirect activity. To know about a thing, is a partial and fragmentary activity. It is a cerebral acrivity which is an indirect activity,
You acquire information about a thing. Knowledge is always an indirect activity. Understanding is a direct action. That is why knowledge has no dynanisn of its own. It has no explosive force of its
own. Knowledge acquired through time and space, through concepts and ideas about a fact, does not lead to any relationship with
reality as it is. It does not lead to any intimate contact with reali-

ty. And what we need is immediate, intimate contact with reality; communion with reality, we need understanding of reality and its movement.

In the immediacy of reality, communion flowers Understanding is the fragrance of that communion. Then your life, your movements, physical, mental, verbal and so on, are simply the result of that understanding. You do not have to do a thing. The understanding acts, the understanding moves, because it is dynamic, it operates upon you, it causes the movement.

Thus we have tried to proceed gradually from the present stuff of our consciousness to the necessity of mutation or transformation to take place within. It is easy for one to know about static things. How can one know about the living humam beings and base one's behaviour on the foundation of that knowledge ? This is a very relevant point·

Is it valid to measure a human being, to judge a human being on the basis of knowledge and experience that one acquires ? Is it warranted ? We judge one another. We compare one human being with another. We compare, we evaluate, we judge and we form opinions and theories about those individuals. This is the activity which goes on in the name of relationship.

Am I entitled to evaluate a human being ? Am I entitled to form an opinion about a human being on the basis of knowledge and authenticity of experience ? What is an experience ? What is knowledge ? A human being is not a static entity. It grows and changes. Every second it can grow and change. It is a living entity.

Knowledge and experience is irrelevant to human relationships. It is very useful where mechanical activities are concerned. It is absolutely necessary when dealing with static objects. Incidentally, there is nothing static even in matter. Thus infomation can be gathered about material things and about patterns of behaviour. How can stored information and stored experiences be valid authority for our relationship with one another ? We will get stuck up in our memory and we will not have relationship with the living human beings at all. We will miss the beauty,

You go to a place, a hill station or the sea—shore. You are tired and for a day or two, you feel rejuvinated; you look at the ocean and it creates an ecstasy; you look at the sunset, the sunrise, and you are thrilled for a day or two. The exhaustion subsides. The nervous stimulation which the contact with the ocean, the sun-set, the hills and the forest, had brought about is over. You get used to the surroundings. The moment you get used to them, the clouds, the birds lose the living relationship. Thus the habit-structure of reacting according to the conditioning and reacting on the basis of knowledge and experience, do not allow us to live and act. Living consists of action. Life is a movement with infinite motion. One has to be terribly sensitive and alert to keep pace with the movement of life, without any inhibition and any fear.

It is not possible to live through the mind. It carries you on the momentum of the sub-conscious; carries you on the momentum of knowledge, experience and motives, i. e. momentum of the past. And being carried over the momentum of knowledge and experience is not living first hand. Being carried over the momentum of instincts is also not living first hand. The addiction to the momentum of thoughts and feelings and motives is not the content of living. The movement of life has a different quality altogether.

One has used self-consciousness; one has used the brain and the mind. Can one go beyond them and act out of an entirely new dimension of consciousness? What makes a human being even imagine that there is something more to human consciousness than the mind, than the brain? We go to bed every day. Imagine that you have had a profound sleep. In the morning, what enables you to say that you have had profound sleep? Because when you sleep, if the sleep is profound, the mind does not obviously function. In a dreamless sound sleep what is awake when the mind sleeps? When you are in a state of love, when all motives go into abeyance by themselves, when thoughts and feelings subside on their own, there is a release of a new sensitivity and energy.

Thus the existence of a different dimension of consciousness than the cerebral activity, than the conscious, the sub-conscious and the unconscious, is not an 'Utopian' idea. It is not an imagination of a visionary person. One gets glimpses of it, provided one is sensitive; provided one is watchful and vigilant about what is happening to oneself. So, there seems to be a dimension of consciousness which is awake, which can function, when the mind does not function. Is it possible to be awake and yet be in a state where the mind does not operate and function ? Is it possible to have the relaxation of profound sleep in waking hours ?

After all meditation is total relaxation that one gets in sleeping hours plus something more. We will come to that 'plus something more', later on. Total relaxation of the mind can be had in the waking hours. That is to say, cessation of mental activity is not paralysis of life or living. People are afraid of cessation of mental activity. Enquiry should not be conducted in any fear. Fear creates many inhibitions. An enquiry conducted under the inhibition of fear is not an enquiry at all. Conducting an enquiry into the unknown needs the relaxation of fearlessness. Thus we should proceed fearlessly. Obviously not through the mind. If I exercise the mind, if, I exercise the ego, the 'I' consciousness, I cannot cross the frontiers. As the mind is let alone, in profound sleep, let it alone in waking hours. Knowing the limitations built-in in its structure, knowing the frontiers constituted by knowledge and experience, we should allow it to be in abeyance.

Knowing the relative field of utility of the mind and brain; using it precisely and accurately in that field and letting it alone when we know that it cannot proceed any further, is the proper way. Time, space, conceptualisation and ideas are of no use any more. So let them alone, spontaneously, out of understanding. If we force the mind into silence, it is no silence at all. If I take a drug of any kind, whether oriental or occidental, and artificially affect the brain-cells and put them to sleep, it is an artificially stimulated, temporary, chemical state. It may give me certain experiences which are extra-sensory, non-sensory or trans-sensory. But it cannot lead to total growth. And we are concerned with the growing of the human race into another dimension of consciousness and not indulging in transcendental and occult experiences. Let them come, if they do. But we are not going to hunt for experiences. Hunting for the pleasure of transcendental and occult experiences is the game of the ambitious ego. It has nothing whatsoever to do with the humility of a spiritual enquiry. It has nothing whatsoever to do with the religious enquiry, the enquiry of what Truth is. If I artificially put the brain-cells to sleep and create a temporary state of quietness, that quietness will not become a dimension of my life. It will not become a soil of my life into which something could flower.

One may use sound-vibrations, a very powerful method and technique. One could study the metaphysics of sound-vibrations; the ancient wise people in the orient have studied it very thoroughly. In India as well as in Tibet, according to the Science of Tantra, the Science of Yoga, every letter has a vibrational range. You could use the vibrational range of various letters and envelop yourself in those vibrations. The sound vibrations have a chemical impact on your body, blood circulation, and the rhythm of breathing, if you have any. You can artificially stimulate a state of quietness through the use of sound vibrations, techniques, or drugs, chemicals, etc. and through concentration.

There are a number of techniques and methods current in the East as well as in the West. A very subtle kind of violence is used against the mind and brain. When I want to force my mind or brain into silence, when I use coercion, or chemicals, am I not using violence on a vary subtle plane ? And how can an enquiry of truth be conducted when I begin with using violence against myself ? The mind will get mutilated. It may be forced into silence. But this use of force leads to mutilation. It has not got the beauty, the subtleness, the freshness and the sharpness of life. It is not intact.

The body and the mind must be intact—fresh llke a rose and tuned in like a violin Silence cannot take place if I use violence against myself. If I understand the limitations of the mind. the built-in deficiencies of the cerebral organ, it is not neceasary to use violence. The challenge facing the human race is to find out ways and means of bringing about a change in a decent and a humane way; a loving and a gentle way and not a violent, barbarious, savage way. The challenge is the same whether you deal with the economic, the political, the cultural, the educational or the religious problems.

Hence forcing the mind into silence and stimulating chemically or neurotically a state of quietness in the mind, is not a spontaneous cessation of mental activity, and no further enquiry can take place unless one arrives at the spontaneous cessation of total mental activity out of understanding the mind,

Thus we have looked at the qualitative difference between the animal consciousness and the complex self-consciousness of the human beings. We have looked at the flourishing of different sciences through the use of self-consciousness. We have looked at the sophistication of tha human brain. We went into the issue of conceptualisation and ideation – the basis of all sciences, natural and social. We also went into the issue of the mind reacting according to the habit-structure, and conditionings, We went very carefully into the issue of what time is. Time and space, which are the two names of one dimension, are inventions of human genius for the convenience of collective behaviour. And we saw logically and scientifically that mankind to-day lives in the realm of concepts and symbols.

There is no harm in living in that realm, provided we are aware that we are in the world of symbols and concepts; and that the concepts and symbols are not Reality. The trouble begins when the symbols are mistaken for reality; when the word is mistaken for the thing it indicates; when the division in psychological time is mistaken for the pure isness of existence. Mistaking symbols for reality is the soil of all manner of bondage. Concepts, symbols are very useful. They have enriched human life. Civilization and culture would not have been possible without them. But these are the decorations of the cerebral structure invented by man. Using a symbol as a symbol, knowing full well its limited utility, and its relative reality, will free you from the bondage of the symbol.

Now we ask ourselves If there is a way of transcending the frontiers of mind. To-morrow we will go into the issue of a non-mental, non-cerebral enquiry. 'Enquiry' is a word that does not satisfy me. Even the word 'discovery' does not satisfy me, because that word has a sense of continuity of an effort. And yet we have to use words from the realm of duality to indicate something that takes place in the realm of nondualiy. I hope you will appreciate the difficulty. Words are loadad heavily with associations, and yet, for verbal communication one has to use the same words.

(27th February, 1971)

Can one come face to face with what is called God or Divinity, Truth or Reality ? God or Divinity has been looked upon as a mental acquisition, as an attainment, achievement; acquisition to be owned and possessed by the individual. And one would like to ask in the very beginning whether there is anything to be attained or achieved in reality; or, is freedom, enlightenment, liberation, only understanding of what is ? People who turn towards religion and spirituality, turn away from the physical, the material, the economic acquisitions. The desire to acquire, the desire to own and possess changes its object from the material, from the physical to the psychological, to the psychic, to the transcendental, to the occult. The ambition to acquire is the same. Whether I want to own a car, a million rupee balance, I want to acquire position and power in society—economic, or political; or, I want to attain transcendental experiences, occult powers, the quality of the mind is the same. The ambition behind these desires is the same. And as far as I can see, the essence of religion is humility.

The essence of religion is renunciation, and I do hope that the word renunciation would not be misunderstood. Renunciation is the austerity to welcome that which life brings to my door-steps, not to reject what life brings and not to seek what is not brought to me; the austerity to walk through the pain and pleasure of life, the austerity to walk through the corridors of insults and flatteries, without getting stuck up anywhere.

So, I would like to turn to-day to the non-cerebral or non-mental enquiry. As long as the mind enquires, the mind will begin its enquiry from the centre of the ego. The consciousness through which we function to-day has a centre that is called 'I', 'the me', 'the ego', as apart from, independent of the consciousness pervading the universe. So, when the 'I' wants to acquire anything, the 'I', the 'me', is one entity, and the world, the life is the other, different from, independent of the so-called 'I' and the 'me'. This duality is there—the 'me' and the 'not-me', the 'I' and the 'not-I'.

The 'I'-consciousness functions in the realm of duality as the subject and object relationship. Without subject and object relationship the 'I'-consciousness cannot function. Whether the object is outside the skin, or the object is inside the skin; in memory of the past experience, or, in the dreams of future, is immaterial. But it needs an object, it needs a motive to stimulate the momentum. So, a mental enquiry cannot take place without strengthening the 'me', the 'ego'.

I want to concentrate, I practise concentration. I practise it intentionally, purposefully. It is a mental activity, and mental activity if done precisely, accurately, sharply and sensitively, will bring about results that are aimed at. If I use certain sound vibrations, use a Mantra and chant it audibly or inaudibly, the 'Vaikhari Japam' or the 'Upamsu Japam', as it is called in the 'Yoga Sutra', the results will be there because it is a mental activity, calculated, programmed, phased out. So, in a mental activity, I know the destination, I have calculated the results. I have projected the results invisibly through my motive. I concentrate upon an idol, an image or a picture of a Guru, a teacher. I focuss all my energy on it; and the identification with that form, with those attributes, will bring about certain chemical changes, certain modifications. So practising concentration is a mental activity having a motive and having a destination, a point of arrival.

There is no point of arrival in life. Life is infinite motion. There is nowhere to reach and nowhere to arrive, but to move without any inhibition whatsoever with the movement of life without getting stuck up anywhere in ideology, in patterns of behaviour, in likes and dislikes, in judgements, in evaluations. It is not easy to live. It is an ordeal. Always to be alert, sensitive, always on one's toes. So, whatever results are achieved through practising concentration, leading to awakening of latent psychic powers, it may have its own uses. But it has nothing whatsoever to do with religion, with spirituality, with the discovery of truth. This has to be understood very clearly.

As I wander around oceans and continents I find that in

the developed countries, the countries that are suffering from affluence, man is turning away from the sensual pleasures, hunting for experiences in the occult and transcendental. Let him hunt. Let him indulge in experience-mongering if he wants to and satisfy his curiosity. Nothing wrong with it. But let him not call it discovery of truth. Let him not call it the essence of religion. There is nothing spiritual about it. So, one has to eliminate every manner of mental activity whose nature we explored yesterday and went into all the lanes and by-lanes of the meehanistic movement of mind; how the mind moves through time and space, how the mind functions with concepts and symbols, how the mind functions only indirectly and has no access, direct and penetrating, to reality. All that we went into step by step yesterday.

Now, to-day, we are going to explore the possibility of a non-cerebral and a non-mental enquiry. How does it take place ? Not through the mind, not through the 'I'–consciousness. Then what does one do with this mind that one uses all the time from morning till night ? The movement of mind, the movement of thought and feeling has been mistaken for the movement of life. We have mistaken the part for the whole, the fragment for the totality. What can one do with the mind ?—That is the question. Before we tackle the mind, as I had mentioned in the second half of my talk yesterday, I would like to go back to that point, we will have to learn to use the mind precisely, accurately, scientifically and we have not been educated to do that. We use varbalisation in a very imbalanced way, unscientific way. We say things which we don't mean. We hide things that we mean. This is an unscientific way of speech. Man has worked hard to develop speech and yet he misuses it. Exaggeration is a sophisticated lie. Understatements, overstatements, unwarranted verbalisation for gossiping, all this is criminal misuse of speech and mind. And if a person indulges in such criminal misuse of mind and speech throughout the day, he cannot hope to arrive at the silence of mind. Suddenly, then he sits down in a corner and closes his eyes. It is not that easy.

One has to learn to use the mind and speech accurately, not to misuse it. Supposing one has leisure, say for a couple of hours a person has nothing to do, no physical activity. He sits in a corner aud goes on brooding, chewing into the experiences of the past. He has no business to violate the modesty of memory, but he does it. He has nothing else to do. So he starts chewing into the experiences of the past. That is misuse of memory. He misuses imagination, dreaming about to-morrows. For actual planning he may use it. but because he has nothing else to do, he goes on daydreaming, misusing the faculty of imagination. This unwarranted inaccurate use or misuse, of mind and speech is the real problem. That is the real culprit, and one has to learn to use this sophisticated, beautiful complex instrument, the cerebral organ, in a sane, scientific and sharp way.

The right kind of relationship with the known will open the doors to the unknown. Unless there is the right kind of relationship with the known, speculation about the unknown will be another trick of the mind, it will be another trick of the ego, and nothing else. If and when we have learnt to use the mind properly, use it when its use is warranted and use it precisely (I can't emphasise it sufficiently); when one has done this, then one is equipped to find out the nature of non-mental or non-cerebral activity. After understanding the whole mechanism of the mind, I say 'the mind connot proceed with me any further'. 'I cannot take the mind with me any further'. So let it alone. Let the mind alone. One has to learn how to let it alone. Before one lets it alone, there is another thing which is worth experimenting. To look at the mind and to observe its movement.

We do not know how to observe. Our moments of perception are contaminated by our subjective reaction. Reactions get mingled in the act of perception. We have lost the elegance of simple perception and spontaneous response. Before I have looked at you, my opinion, my likes and dislikes about human beings, their figures, their shapes, the colour of their skin, the way they walk around—all those likes and dislikes and opinions come up and with electronic speed they get mingled into the act of perception. So I do not see the fact of you. I see the fact of you coloured by my decision, by my judgement, by my opinion, by my preference or prejudice. Observation is so difficult to arrive at.

One has to learn to observe. If one cannot observe the movement of the mind, then what is going to take place beyond mind
will not be observed. So one has to learn to observe the movement
of the mind. As one observes the clouds in the sky, the flowers
in a garden, the ripples on the waters, the waves on the ocean,
as one observes without wanting to do anything about them, one
observes easily in a relaxed way; so to observe the movement
of mind in a relaxed way, without condemning, without accepting,
without denying. First one observes it, sitting by oneself in solitude
and if this state of observation can be sustained in solitude then
one can be in the state of observation throughout the day. One
goes to office to work, listens to the words of the boss, sees the
reaction coming up in oneself, of anger, of irritation, of annoyance.
One sees the objective challenge and the subjective reaction coming
up simultaneously. And this capacity to be aware of the objective
challenge and the subjective reactions simultaneously results in a
take-off of consciousness from the plane of challenge and reaction
to a different plane altogether.

Subjective reactions exposed to the light of attention and
awareness lose the grip on you. They are there. But they lose the
hold on you, they lose the grip on you, they lose the power to
distort and twist your responses. So observation without any conscious effort on the part of the individual, sustained observation
results in a qualitatively new awareness with which one can live
and move. Cook a meal, scrub the floor, wash the floor, work in
the office, meet the situations of life. So the learning of
observation is an equipment necessary for the non-mental and
non-cerebral enquiry. One has to learn this. And we have not learnt
it in schools and colleges.

Nowhere, in no country of the East and the West, are
children helped to understand their minds. They are taught Physics, Chemistry, Biology, and all the subjects. But they are not
introduceed to their own minds. they are not taught the chemistry
of emotion, they are not taught to see the nervous tension that the
movement of thought brings about. And what the tensions do to
the children ? What those chemical pressures do to them ? I do
hope some day humanity will realise, and earlier the day comes

the better for humanity. That acquaintance with mind should be introduced, incorporated in the study, in the educational progamme, in all the schools; so that by the time a child comes out of his higher secondary exemination, the matriculation, or by the time he goes to University, he is acquainted with his mind. The mind is no more a mystery to him.

The mind has been looked upon as something mysterious; the sub-conscious, the unconscious, something to be afraid of. Half a century ago people went to religious teachers and preachers to consult about the mental and psycholoical problems; and now-a-days, people go to psycho-analysts, psychiatrists, psychologists. They had relegated the power half a century ago to priests and preachers and now the power is vested in psychologists, psycho-analysts and psychiatrists, as if man is not mature enough in the second half of the twentieth century to deal with his own mind. He can talk about world peace. He can land on the moon. But his own mind,—no it is not his subject.

These intermediaries between the reality of your own life and yourself will have to be eliminated, and man will have to shoulder the responsibility of handling his cerebral organ on his own and I feel man is born to do that. There is nothing mysterious about it The only thing is, one has to begin anew, look afresh at the whole issue of human life. If you say that anger and jealousy and envy are human nature, the desire to dominate, to own,-to possess, are human nature; then man is doomed to live in a society cluttered with exploitation and violence. As far as the speaker is concerned, I do not think man is doomed to live on that way. Man has to become mature and learn to live in love and friendship, peace and justice. And they will come not as a dream or a vision, but the revolt of the young generation the world over tells me in very plain terms that the day will not be far off.

So sustained observation throughout the day, and in daily relationships will help human beings to grow into a qualitatively different awareness. To be aware of the objective challenge and the subjective reaction simultaneously, to take them both in one sweep of glance, in one sweep of attention, one sweep of awareness. When that is done, then letting the mind alone will not be a problem. The mind can spontaneously, without any resistance, be quiet, when we are fully aware that it cannot proceed any further, that ideation, conceptualisation are of no use in the realm of reality, in the realm of non-duality. Then of its own accord, mind becomes quiet. There is no movement of thoughts, no movement of emotions. I do hope, we realise what it means.

When I think a thought, there is a dual movement going on within me. When I think a thought, that thought leads to a kind of nervous tension, irrespective whether the thought is good or bad according to you. Nervous tension resulting from thought will be the same, and the emotional content of that will stimulate a chemical pressure in the body. So the nervous tension and chemical pressure, these are the two results which accompany thought. Thought is a vibration, and the moment there is a vibration inside you, it affects your breathing, it affects the blood circulation. it creates a nervous tension and it results in a chemical pressure. Look, whether you verbalise the thought to yourself audibly or not, of course, the thought is there with the words. For the fun of it, one can experiment and find out if there be a thought which is not clothed in sound vibrations. And what does the movement of a thought within you do to your whole being ? To be sensitive to the movement. So with every thought that comes up, with every emotion that comes up there is a jerk given to the breathing system, there is a jerk in the blood circulation.

Nervous tension and chemical pressure are bound to accompany every thought that you think, every emotion you feel. That is how energy is consumed. You may sit in a room quietly for an hour. You feel you are not doing any work, but the mind wanders about. It thinks, it feels. it reacts, it broods, it worries and at the end of the hour you are more tired than a person who has walked four miles in that hour, because vital energy is consumed mith the movement of thoughts and emotions. That is a physical fact. It is not a theory that I am communicating to you. So when the mind has become quiet, there are no vibrations giving jerks to the breathing system, to the blood circulation. When there is no tension of any manner, when there is no pressure of any manner, there is a state of total relaxation.

The state of silence is a state of relaxation which is not a negative state. It appears to be negative, it appears to be empty, but the emptiness of silence is like the emptiness of the space which is full of creative forces. So that state of relaxation, that state of silence, comes to life, not as an experience of the mind, Any experience of the mind is in the mental sphere. It is in the realm of duality. That which can be recognised, that which can be identified, that which can be experienced, is still the game of the ego, of the ' I '-consciousness, So silence that is experienced by the mind is not a dimension of which we are talking. Every experience has its own tensions, painful or pleasurable, but the tensions are the same. So, there is a state of total relaxation when the energy at the root of our existence gets an opportunity for the first time to return to its own source and be there in its totality. The energy that was scattered and dissipated all over the place gets an opportunity to return to the navel point in the body, in the human organism and be there in its totality, in its wholeness,

We do not know to-day what the totality of energy means. We have been riding on the momentum of motives, wishes, ambitions. We know only the motion of the motive, the speed of the motive. We have been riding the momentum of a thought, of an emotion, That is all fragmentary and partial movement. So we do not know the movement of totality. We cannot speculate about it. But in that state of total relaxation, energy for the first time gets an opportunity to be whole. And energy is not static. It is infinite motion. It has motion which cannot be measured by the mind, and that infinite motion begins to function, begins to operate upon the whole individual. There is no ' I '-consciousness to do something with that state. But it is the totality of energy, which is moving now, which is operating. Not the I, but the it. It begins to operate now. It begins to move.

If you love music you might have noted what happens when you listen to a concert or to a piece of classical music. When you listen to music, do you listen only with your ear ? Or, does the whole being listen, from the crown of your head to the toes of your feet ? The act of listening vibrates through the whole being, and there is a communion not only with the notes of music. but even with the interval between two notes. The sensitivity of the whole being has a communion with the silence between the two notes as well as with the overtones and under-tones of each note. It is an event to listen to music. If you listen only with the ears, wanting to compare with Beethoven's 9th symphony, what happens ? Is it better than the second ? Is it worse than the ninth ? And how did the Austrian orchestra play it and how did some-one conduct it ? Then you are listening only with the brain, with the ears and not with your whole being. But if you are in love with music, then the whole being listens. That is to say, the sensitivity of the whole being functions, After all sensitivity, intelligence, love, they are not located at one point in the human organism. They permeate the whole being as energy permeates the whole universe. So listening to music becomes an event of communion of the whole being with something.

When you are in love, then the whole being is communicated. The sensitivity of the whole being becomes operative in the egoless state of love. In the same way, in the total relaxation, in the state of sustained silence, the wholeness of energy, the totality of energy begins to operate. In other words, intelligence which is sensitivity, which is love, begins to operate. A different kind of perception is born. That is why I said the other day, silence as a dimension of consciousness comes to life, if the state of total relaxation is sustained. It is difficult to be in real state of total relaxation because as soon as you find yourself in that state, for sometime, for a fraction of a minute, for a couple of minutes, the ego that was in abeyance comes back with a jump and says, "What is this ? nothing to do, I can't do anything, I can't move, there is no direction to go, there is nothing to observe, this is a bottomless pit, this is darkness, run away from this place." As soon as the state of total relaxation or silence is suspended for a minute or two, the 'I'-consciousness that was in abeyance jumps back on you with a vengeance and says—"what are you doing here ? Nowhere to go and nothing to do. I will die, this is a bottomless pit, turn back, turn away." This is the 'dark night of the soul' and people want to run away from that state of inaction. It is not a state of inactivity. Activity and inactivity are obverse and converse of the same thing. This is total non-action. So that is the last struggle of the 'I'-consciousness, last attempt of the ego, to come back and trap you, saying "this is dreadful, this is dark."

If one does not turn away, if one is not frightened by the reaction of the ego, it will make you weak, it will make you feel suffocated, it will make you feel uneasy. If one is aware that all these tears and suffocation are the reactions of the clever ego, then one sticks it out, one puts one stick into it and remains with that apparent emptiness, remains in that apparent bottomless pit. Where there is nothing to do, to be in the state of non–doing, to be in the state of total relaxation, We are going step by step. If and when that is done, then the intelligence and the sensitivity which were blocked by cerebral movement, which were blocked by knowledge and experience, get released. In the state of egolessness the non–dual perception and the non–dual response as a new quality begins to manifest itself.

Yesterday, we saw how from the simple consciousness of the animal world man emerged with the capacity of self–consciousness. Now in that state of total relaxation, a new quality of non-dual perception and a non-dual response begins to manifest. A new quality of intelligence begins to function. This will sound something Utopian. This will sound something visionary; and I can understand if it is felt visionary. The only thing that I can do is to tell you in all humility that it is only a statement of what happens in life. Duality and all the conflicts and tensions that we are acquainted with, is only a fragment of that huge immense life. So the individual is there. The same individual, the same form is there,—the flesh and the bone. But it is egolessness clothed in flesh and bone. It is receptivity and humility clothed in flesh and bone, as you have emptiness clothed in the drums that you play upon.

Thus the state of total relaxation results in receptivity. Sensitivity is to be eternally in receptivity, uninhibited receptivity. Receptivity uninhibited by knowledge, by the arrogance of experience. Then only one can learn. To-day we have been educated in the acquisitive and additive process of knowledge. Go on adding, piece by piece, bit by bit, to your knowledge, to your experiences. Knowing is an additive and acquisitive process. We do not know how to

3

learn. But then in that state of humility one is always in the state of learning. To receive, to learn, to perceive, to observe—that's a total action and that state of total action is the state in which discovery of the meaning of life can take place. Relaxed in the realm of non-duality, relaxed in the totality of energy, relaxed in the receptivity and humility,—one can then perceive that which 'is'.

To-day, we cannot perceive what 'is'. We impose ourselves on the unit of perception through our values, our ideas, our ideologies. Thought and emotion has been organised, standardised and regimented through centuries. This subjective imposition upon the objective facts, the malady from which we suffer to-day will not be there. I wonder if you have noticed as I have that thought has been organised and regimented, systematised. That is why one fact is interpreted by the Hindus in one way and the same fact is interpeted by the Muslims in just the opposite way. A fact is interpreted by a Catholic in one way and the Communist interprets the same fact in a diametrically opposite way. This collective interpretation of the facts and reacting to those interpretations collectively would not have been possible if thought had not been regimented, if emotions had not been regimented, if they had not been standardised in the name of religion, culture, and civilisation.

Political thought has been organised, economic thought has been organised, regimented, and, therefore, the initiative of the individual is lost. And man has to regain that freedom in all fields of activity, at all levels of consciousness, without being afraid of anything whatsoever, and least of all of God. So, beyond the field and area of organised thought and emotion, beyond the frontiers of all the crystallised patterns and ways of behaviour, there is the realm of non-duality, tremendous sensitivity and intelligence which has a different perception from that of the brain.

Man has to move. You might have noticed how a mother understands the need of the child without the child verbalising it. The sensitivity of her love for the child gives her the capacity to perceive directly without the intervention of the mind. Without the intervention of the idea, the mother has an access to what is happening within the child. The sensitivity, the intelligence give her a different kind of perception. When you love a person in the limited sense of the word love, that love releases a new kind of intelligence, a new kind of sensitivity by which you feel the needs of the person you love without his or her verbalisation about them. It is a kind of direct and immediate contact with reality. The intervention of mind beɔomes unnecessary. Verbalisation, ideation becomes unwarranted. Time and space get eliminated in the state of love. Whether it is love between two friends, love between a man and a woman, love between a mother and a child, motives are eliminated, emotions get eliminated, ego gets effaced; it is at least held in abeyance in that relation. So the release of a tremendously intense sensivity, release of a new intelligence altogether is there all the time. And it operates. That's a dimension, and I feel man has to grow into that dimension, live there and move out of that dimension, use the body and the mind out of that dimension of intelligence.

Man has been using the dimension of cerebral movement. In the 18th and 19th century, or, rather from the days of renaissance in Europe, man has looked upon himself as a rational animal. But reason is not the only discriminating factor. It seems to me that intelligence and love are the discriminating factors for species of the human animal. He has not become mature. He is still raw. Please excuse me if you find these words arrogant. But had not man been raw and immature. there would not be so many wars, there would not be violence and aggressions. Not only in the battle-fields but also in the family, day and night there is aggression, injustice, jealousy, suspicion,—wife suspecting the husband, husband suspecting the wife, parents wanting to dominate over the childern, the children wanting to deny the parents. This game of acquisition, ownership and possession. not only in the economic and material fields but also in the psychological fields is going on day and night, and as long as man is a prisoner of his own mind, injustice and exploitation, aggression and violence will never be eliminated from human life.

One will have to grow into the maturity of intelligence, maturity of love; and love and intelligence exist beyond the frontiers of mind. That is why this non-mental, the non-cerebral enquiry taking place in the cessation of mental movement, taking place in the relaxation of the total being, taking place in the dimension of silence not conducted by the individual, but brought about by silence, is urgently needed today. A handful revolutionaries, who feel concerned about the state of human affairs existing in the world to-day are needed to explore what takes place beyond the frontiers of mind, beyond the frontiers of cerebral movement, to explore it factually in their own lives.

To-morow evening, we will take up the issue whether one needs a guide for these things. What is a guide ? What is a master ? What is a Guru ? Or, what is a disciple or a Chela or a pupil ? Is a guide necessary? And what kind of relationship can exist between a person who has transcended the frontiers of mind and lives there? What kind of relationship can exist between that person and the rest of the human beings ? So the question of master and disciple relationship will be taken up to-morrow evening.

Again, I would like to thank each one of you, who has been kind enough to come and attend the second talk of the series. I think the people of Ceylon are giving me a great surprise by attending the talks of an utter stranger who has no claims of any authority, who is not a 'Yogi', not a 'Sanyasi', not a saint, not a spiritual teacher, who has not come here to propagate anything. To come to listen to an absolutely ordinary human being who is one of you. is extremely kind of you and credit goes also to the organisers.

•

: 4 :

(28th February, 1971)

How does an enquirer set about the personal discovery of truth ? Where and how does an enquirer begin ? Does he go about and go round to find out someone who will guide him, who will instruct him, who will carry him towards God, towards Truth, who will protect him against the odds which are bound to be on the path of the unknown ? Does an enquirer begin with hunting for a Guru, for a master, for a teacher ? Is it inevitable ? And who is to tell him that a certain person is liberated, is free, is illumined ? Has he to accept the sanctions of people, of books ? How does this whole thing begin? I wonder if you have ever thought about the issue. Why do I go out and why do I seek a teacher or a master ? What makes me look out for and search for a master ?

We will go into what the master is or a teacher is, later on. But what makes me go and look for one ? Is it that I am afraid ? Is it that I do not want to take a risk ? I have been taught to earn money, to own it, to possess it, to have a house, to have a bank balance, to have social recognition and prestige as a security. I have known economic security, political security; psychological security and now I want to begin my enquiry after having been assured of some kind of transcendental security. Is it my urge for security that makes me look out for a teacher or a master ? Am I afraid of the unknown ? Am I afraid of God or Divinity ? Am I afraid of freedom ? Is it the fear of freedom, fear of the unknown that pushes me and obliges me to find out someone who will hold my finger and carry me securely and safely from the known to the unknown ? If it is the urge for security in the very process of discovery, if it is the fear of freedom or unknown, then am I really in a state, a proper state, to conduct an enquiry ? Fear creates its own inhibitions. We are a fear-ridden humanity to-day. We are suffering from chronic fear. That is the malady which is at the root of many ills existing in society. So, fear creates its own inhibitions and the urge for security creates its own reservations. So I will have to find out if I am looking out for a teacher because I am afraid of freedom. What will happen if the sense of belonging to a family, to a community, to a country, to a race, whithers away like the autumn leaves ? What will happen if the 'I'-consciousness, the ego, at the centre of my being gets effaced completely ? What will happen to me ?

On one hand we want to enquire, to find out what the ultimate Truth is and on the other hand, we want to be secure. And in the name of religion and spirituality, human beings go on balancing these two parallel currents in their own life. An enquiry which begins in fear, is no enquiry at all. An enquiry which wants secu rity at the same time, is not a scientific enquiry. Unless one has the courage to be vulnerable in life, unless one has the intensity or the urge to find out what truth is, to learn what life is, to find out what death is, the beauty of that magnificent event that is called death, real enquiry cannot begin. Unless that urge is there which melts away all fear, which whithers away all reservations, personal discovery cannot take place.

Intellectual acquisition of theories and ideas, of ideologies, does not need any courage. It is a mechanistic activity that can be safely conducted. But personal discovery of truth, which is the essence of religion, needs tremendous energy and fearlessness. It needs courage. Freedom and enlightenment are not the game of the cowards. So one has to find out for oneself whether one is afraid of what one is going to find out. And when one is afraid, then one needs blueprints, one needs calculated results, one needs the assurance that at each step he would be able to measure his own progress, compare it with the progress of other people, evaluate himself in his own eyes as well as in the eyes of other people and go on as he moves on in a college or university measuring his progress, measuring his attainments and achievements. Unfortunately, that does not happen in life,

This contradictiou of finding out what truth is, what freedom is and simultaneously the desire to be secure, the desire to be protected, has got to be resolved in the very beginning. Otherwise the desire for security and protection will compel us to gathe , to borrow experiences of other people—occult, trsncendental or any other kind of experiences, to borrow their words, to borrow their experiences and try to approximate our lives to their experiences. Fear will make us accept the authority of another individual or individuals, books, scriptures, and so on. And the moment one has accepted the authority in the very beginning, discovery comes to an end. The beauty of life is that neither enqu,ry nor freedom can ever be borrowed. Knowledgc can be borrowed, but truth can never be borrowed, Borrowed words, phrases, experiences do not transmit life and energy. That is one aspect about which one has to be careful.

Secondly, even if I want to find and look out for a teacher or a master. how do we konw, who is a teacher, who is a master ? What is a Guru or a master ? This term is used in India, in Sanskrit literature of the ancient days. What does it mean ? Is it a description of an individual ? Or. is it a symbol for a state of consciousness expressed through an individual ? The word Guru indicates a state of consciousness from which all manner of ignorance has been dispelled completely. A person who lives in a state of consciousness, which is unconditionally free, which is sensitive, is a Guru. The infinite motion of sensitivity is love and he is the embodiment of love. So he is a person from whose consciousness all manner of ignorance, all manner of bondage, has been eliminated altogether, a person who has transcended the frontiers of the ego, the 'I'- consciousness. A person who lives in the state of nothingness, is "nothin gness", as we said last evening, clothed in flesh and bone. There is no one there to assert that "I have experienced", "I have become free". There is no one to assert that 'I can teach you', no one to assert that "I can be your guide". There is no one who can demand anything of you, who would like to influence you, to convert you, even to convince you,

Truth is for living, not for asserting. It is only when the experience gets contaminated by the 'I'-consciousess, that the desire to assert creeps in. The desire to convince and convert others is an indication of the ego. So when a person transcends the frontiers of the conditioned hrain, when a person has grown into an entirely new dimension of consciousness, which has no centre and no perihpery at all, who is there to assert ? With whom are you going to have a static relationship and say that "this is my master and I am his pupil" ? Beyond the frontiers of mind there is no time and space, there is the infinite motion of sensitivity, infinite motion of awareness. the quality of which we do not know to-day. We know the momentum of thoughts, we know the momentum of feelings, motives, we do not know the infinite motion of life, we do not know the momentum of silence, which has a tremendous momentum, which has a dynamism of its own, which is a dimension of life, full of creative force as the space is full of life.

Thus beyond the frontiers of mind the person is living in limitless sensitivity, living in the dynamic motion of love and awareness, How are you going to arrest the movement of that person's life and bind him in a static relationship, to claim—"here is my Guru", "here is my master" ? You cannot capture the breeze that comes to you, in your fist, and say "this is my breeze !" Even if there is such a person and yon come across him, or life brings him across your path, how are you going to arrest him in time, in temporal, psychological relationship ? How are you going to impose psychological relationship on a person who has become nothingness, because there is no ego, there is no 'I'-consciousness ? It is the universal consciousness blowing through that individual and singing the song through that flesh and those bones. So the individual is no more there.

Relationship needs two static points. I can be related to this microphone. It is there. It has been there for the last fifteen minutes. It will be there for the next forty-five minutes. So I can place myself in a position, in an angle, at a distance where I can specify the relationship with the microphone, with that door, with those walls. You can have relationship with the people who are living within the frontiers of mind. who have the centre of the 'I' consciousness, because thought and emotion which are the product of collective human activity, are the same in you and in them. So within the frontiers of mind and brain, the so-called relationships that we know are possible. But beyond them, can there be a relationship ? I would like to attract your attention to this very fundamental issue.

Secondly, can an enquirer be static ? As the state of freedom is a dynamic state, constantly movng, in the same way, is not enquiry also a dynamic movement going on within a person ? And can an enquirer be an enquirer for the rest of his life ? And is an enquirer an enquirer throughout the twenty-four hours ? Does rhe integrity of enquiry remain with us even throughout the waking hours ? It remains for an hour or so when we listen to a talk, It is there when we visit the temple, the mosque, the monastery. Even there for how much time the attitude of enquiry, the unconditional receptivity, the humility is there, is something to be discovered by oneself. May be out of the one hour that we are in the hall, the state of enquiry, the state of receptivity is there only for a few minutes. So one is an enquirer only when the integrity of enquiry is alive, not otherwise. We are under an illusion that we are enquirers and 'Jijnasus' and 'Sadhakas'. We are not. The state of enquiry is not sustained even through the ten or twelve waking hours, leave aside the hours of sleep. The state of enquiry can be sustained throughout waking hours only when we relate the enquiry to everything that we do from morning till night, to correlate enquiry of truth to everything that we do.

You know, it is a hard job. As an enquirer you cannot accept anything because it has been a tradition, because you have read, because you have heard about. You have to test everything for yourself, find out the validity for yourself. Nobody likes to do that. To be alert, sensitive, to question the validity of everything that has been thought and handed down through traditions, through culture whether it is economic, political, cultural, religious or spiritual, is not an easy thing. To question the validity of everything that has come, needs tremendous humility.

To-day is the age of revolt. To-day is the age of rejection. Revolting and rejecting is not what I imply at all. Let me make my point very clear. Acceptance and rejection are the obverse and converse of the same thing. The quality of mind is the same, whether you accept it without testing the validity or you reject it without questioning the validity. Blind acceptance and blind rejection, nothing to choose between them. So, it needs tremendous humility and fearlessness to question the validity of everything. Not to do anything out of habit-structure not to do anything repetitively, mechanistically, To find out the content of my relationship with my shoes, with my clothes, with the food that I eat, the house, the furniture that I use, is the content of enquiry. When an enquiry gets correlated with the totality of life, then only a person can be called a 'Sadhaka' or a real enquirer, a genuine enquirer. But we have fragmented life into individual life and collective life, secular life and religious life, mundane life and.spiritual life. We have divided life into economic and political life and we have developed sets of values for each division,each fragment.

We have codes of conduct for each compartment of life. And the sets of values may be mutually incompatible. They may be inconsistent with one another. But we live according to them. These are the economic values, these are the political values, this is the tradition of the family. So we go on nourishing in our person contradictory, inconsistent sets of values and the pathetic efforts to live according to the inconsistent codes of conduct are appalling ! ! And that's why man gets torn within. Man with capital 'M' has become a split personality. He is suffering from skizofrania all the world over, whether we are in the starvation-stricken countries or we are in the affluence-stricken countries. So one would like to point out in all humility that it is no joke to be an enquirer. It is a no joke to find out what Truth is and what Reality is.

You cannot buy Truth or Reality with the currency of a handful, a number of transcendental and occult powers. The currency of powers and experiences does not work here. You cannot purchase. It is not a commercial commodity. So, one has to find out whether one lives in the state of sustained enquiry, whether one has the courage to correlate the enquiry of truth to everything that one does from morning till night, physically, verbally cerebrally, and so on. This correlation of enquiry of truth to the totality of life intensifies the enquiry. It goes on becoming deeper. It percolates through all the layers of being, and your whole life becomes a living flame of that enquiry. You are not different from that enquiry any more. You are consumed by that enquiry all the time. And as there is a law of gravitation, which controls physical body, as there is a law of causation that governs the cerebral movement,—there is also a law of love. And as a piece of magnet attracts a piece of iron, in the same way, the state of freedom, wherever it might have been attained or arrived at, attracts this flame of enquiry, wherever it is located in any person, in any country, in any part of the world.

It is the state of enquiry meeting the state of freedom which could be called the meeting of a teacher and a pupil, the master and disciple. If it is only for a fraction of a second then the meeting has taken place only for a fraction of a second. When the state of enquiry is not there, the person may be sitting and living withot any light for the rest of the life. Nothing will happen because the body is like a vessel containing that state of consciousness. And unless one has a direct contact with the state of consciousness, nothing can take place, no change can take place. Thus when there is a meeting between enquiry and freedom, enquiry and understanding through two persons, a phenomenon takes place like the positive and the negative wires of electricity coming together.

Instead of hunting outside, therefore, instead of looking for masters and teachers, searching for them, it seems to me quite scientific, sane, and also safe, that one turns inwards and finds out if the love for freedom, the love for understanding, for enlightenment, has become a basic need of life. As the enquiry goes on ripening within, and as it goes on becoming mature, the maturity of the enquiry explodes into understanding. Life is bound to bring such an enquirer near a person, an individual, who might be living in the state of freedom, unconditional freedom.

Thus the word Guru cannot be imposed permanently upon a person. It indicates a state of consciousness. And the word disciple or a 'Sisya' or a 'Chela' also indicates a state of enquiry, receptivity. And receptivity attracts love and freedom as the scorched earth after the summer season attracts the rains and gets new life when the clouds descend and bathe the earth with the waters of life. It has got to happen. An enquirer can never be lonely. He does not have to worry who is going to guide him or instruct him. Leave that to Life. Leave that to the law of love. Be concerned with the honesty, the integrity and the intensity of your own enquiry, correlate it with all the life and leave the rest to life itself.

This is not being said in the sense of fatalism. But life is immense. The life that we catch between the two points of birth and death is not the only life. And the intellect, the brain, the mind cannot uncover the mystery of life. The brain has its own limitations that we have seen yesterday. So, instead of searching with the help of the disturbed mind, ambitious mind, frustrated mind, instead of hunting with that mind, it seems to be warranted and desirable both, to turn inward and pay more attention to the nature of enquiry that one has. "Do I want to find out what Truth is ? Is finding out the meaning of life the top priority of my life ? Why do I want to find it ?"—these questions are very relevant.

Purification of the enquiry, through observing its nature, in the thing that one can do. One can do something about it: And this is being said in great agony because wandering through various countries and continents of this globe, one comes across individuals who have converted spiritual and religious matters into commercial propositions. They want to propagate, they want to capture people, they want to sell occult experiences, they want to sell Mantras and tender young men and women who have seen the limitations of sensual pleasure, who have seen the limitations of mental pleasures and pains, who are bored with the mediocrisy of affluence, are turning more and more towards them. They also feel that they can buy religion, they can buy Truth and Reality. So, without criticising any one (criticism has no value) with all the humility, pain and agony that a sensitive lover of humanity can feel, I am sharing this with you that if one goes out with frustration, ambition, disturbance—emotional or intellectual, one will be victimised. So one should beware.

The third point I would like to share with you this evening on this very basic issue, is that one might come across an individual and learn from his life, learn from the expression of freedom and enlightenment through his being. Does that entitle one to limit one's discovery to the total way of living of that individual ? Individuals may be great. But Truth is greater. Life is greater than individuals. So, am I entitled, as an enquirer of truth, as a person wanting to discover the meaning of life, to limit the meaning of life, the content of freedom, of liberation or enlightenment ? Can I limit it with the experiences of that particular individual ? It is a very important question. If I limit the content of truth, the content of freedom, by the life of that person, then I will become dogmatic. That is how sects are born. Not knowing how to punish great men for their greatness, fate punishes them with their disciples. I limit the truth with the life of that person and then I claim him as my master, your master, my God, your God. We start comparing them, claiming superiority. Now that the whole play of the ego comes in, enquiry is brushed aside. I want to show to the world that my master or my teacher is better than yours.

In the name of religion and spirituality, the vulgar play of ego-centred activity comes to the forefront. And beeause it is done in the name of spirituality we do not hesitate, we give full play, full display. So, this competition, this assertion, this dogmatism, this whole hid-eous game, goes on and you can imagine the pain of a person who has been born and brought up in India and who has had to witness all this—not second hand, but first hand, right from Kanyakumari to the Himalayas, to the shores of the Ganges where one has gone personally, not from the books. So there are two evil things that result from this tendency of limiting the Truth by the person. First, the enquiry within me stops and secondly, the dogmatism, the propagandist mentality, takes over. We become more interested in spreading the word, in propagating the word, in repeating it rather than living it. So, in the evening of life, at the end of our life, we have only the ashes of empty words and empty shells in our hands, but not the light of life or truth. Truth is for living, not for propagating. It will express itself, it has got the dynamic force to express itself in spite of you.

The fourth point that one would like to share with friends is that when one comes in contact with such a person, if at all one comes across, what does one see ? Suppose the person is beautiful, is handsome, as it is bound to be in a way, because the inner beauty of Truth radiates through the physical form. The physical form becomes resplendent with the beauty of Truth and Love. If the person is beautiful or handsome, our sensuality gets attracted by the beauty of the form and, instead of penetrating any further, the beauty of the form, the shape, the aesthetic sense block our way. We start imitating that, we get attached to that. That beauty stimulates.

And when the person ia away from us, then the enquiry goes into slumber. It becomes passive. It loses its initiative. It loses its momentum. So we become addicted to the presence, Please do see this. We become addicted to the presence. There is nothing wrong in feeling elevated when one is in the presence of a beautiful or handsome person. But one gets attached to it, attracted, then infatuated, then depenent upon that beauty for stimulating the enquiry, then one gets addicted.

Those who are more sophisticated, more sensitive. penetrate through the beauty or ugliness of the form, the crudeness or the refinement of the form and they come face to face with the lucidity of expression, with the clarity of vision. with the poetic diction, with the music of the voice, the presentation and so on. They get attracted intellectually and emotionally. And intellectually one captures those expressions, those words. It is eaay because we are used to doing that, we have been trained to do that in the universities. Intellectual grabbing of things, acquiring them is not very difficult It has become the way of our life. So we get attached to the thoughts. By listening to the talks or reading the books we can formulate a way of living, a pattern of thinking, a pattern of reacting. So if the person is saying "do not conform to anything, do not impose. any discipline"; then revolting against discipline, revolting against conformism comes about, In other words, non conformism becomes again a sect for us becau'se we have not gone through that. We are only imitating. we are trying to conform to the non conformism.

Intellectual or psychological addiction to the way of thinking or presentation of that person becomes our vested interest. Look at the pitfalls on the path of self-discovery. One needs the austerity of awareness, right from the first moment till the last. One needs the austerity of freedom, not to depend opon the form, whether it is the foim of the body or the form of the word, not to become dependent upon; and to emotionally adore, intellectually worship. Politically, we like to worship heroes, leaders. Whether we are in a democratic country or a dictatorial country, this hero worship is there. Psychologically, adoring, admiring and worshipping is easy, because the moment we worship, we relegate our responsibiity to that person, to lead us. It becomes easy for us, Unless one is willing to shoulder the responsibility of living first hand, in total freedom, self-discovery cannot take place. So one has to be very aware not to get stuck. To have the state of sustained enquiry, to be in that state of intense enquiry is the only thing that man can do and has got to do. To remain in that intense enquiry, without getting dependent anywhere, without seeking protection and security anywhere, to be vulnerable throughout, that is the most important thing.

We have been told through centuries that freedom is a destination where you can arrive and then you can rest and relax, as if liberation, illumination are static points in life, as if there is nothing more to do then. There is no static point in life. Life is infinite motion. Life is eternal dynamism; and to live is to be free to move with the movement of life spontaneously without any inhibition, without any fear. To live is to move with the movement of life — inside you and outside you, in harmony. So, one cannot get stuck up in destinations, in arrivals, in protections, in guidance.

One has to learn; not that one does not learn from life, not that one does not learn from those who have gone before. You and I are not the first enquirers of truth. There have been many in all parts of the world. One has to learn from them. But learning is not an additive or acquisitive process. When you walk on a road and you see a sign-post and see the direction of the rord, you read the sign-post, but you do not cling to it, you do not embrace it and say "O my darling I will be with you" You read the contents, and you walk ahead. Similarly, you learn from life at large, from birds, from trees, from plants, from children, from every individual and specially from those who have had the courage to transcend the frontiers of this limited human brain, who are living in a state of consciousness where there is no centre and no periphery. They do emanate peace, love, joy.

When you go to a garden, even without your touching the flowers and claiming them to be your own, the beauty, the fragrance, the perfume of the flowers does something to you. So to be in the presence of individuals who are really living first hand, and not second hand, through ideas or ideologies, is bound to send you in ecstasy. It is bound to do something to you. It is a physical fact. The transformation that takes place in the company of an individual who has grown into the maturity of egolessness, who has grown into the maturity of silence and lives there, whose words are only the shadow of silence, whose words are made of the substance of that silence within, whose physical movements are the expressions of inner peace ! When one is there, one will learn. One will grow into a different quality of consciousness. But that is not your doing or my doing. It is a happeniug. It is an event that takes place.

Transformation is never born of your achievement or attainment. Illumination or liberation is an event that takes place in life when enquiry and illumination blend together as a blessing of life But the petty little mind cannot acquire it, own it, attain it.

Thus this evening we have looked at certain basic issues. We began with saying that if the enquiry is born of fear or the urge for security, it will not lead to any discovery at all. It will be a mental activity, it will be an ego-centred activity. Man has emerged with a new quality of consciousness, viz. self-consciousness. But the fear and the urge for security that he has brought over from the animal life with him, still dominates his being. The urge for security and the fear of life or the physical level has some role to play. One has to defend oneself against the weather, climate, wild animals, and so on.

The urge for security has a role to play as far as the physiologieal life is concerned. But this fear has been carried over to the psychological realm and we meet one another in fear. We want to guard ourselves against the others. We want to guard ourselves against the movement of life psycholgically; and we create the concept of time, the symbol of time as to-day, tomorrow, yesterday. This addiction to these symbols, added to the fear and urge for security, plays havoc on our life. So, one has to find out if it is valid to carry the urge for security to the psychological realm in human relationships. And as long as you and I meet in fear, as long as I meet the moment, the present moment that life presents to me, the now, the here, in fear, can there be a communion between life and myself ?

It seems to me that carrying over the urge for security and fear to the psychological realm is a mistake on the part of the human being. It is something unscientific, and one carries this and the urge for security even in a religious quest, even in a quest for ultimate truth—and that contaminat-es the nature of enquiry and that contaminates the nature of discovery.

Perhaps during the stay in Ceylon, in one of the meetings, I might take up the issue what is fear ? What is the urge for security ? How is it connected with thought and time ? We might take it up one day, not to-day. But I was going to point out that any enquiry conducted in fear and goaded by the urge for security is not going to take us very far in self-discovery. The mind will find out something or someone that suits it emotionally. I have my emotional idiosyncrasies. So I will find out a person who suits me emotionally. Or, if I am addicted to the cerebral movement, addicted to certain ideas and ideologies, then I find out a person whose thoughts and ways of expressing those thoughts is nearer to my thinking. So the urge for security will not help me find out who the teacher is, will not help me to find out what the meaning of life is. So one must find out in the very beginning—"Am I willing to pay the price of insecurity ? Do I want to find out what truth is, what freedom is, at the cost, the price that I will have to pay ?"

Enquiry is not a path of roses. It is not walking through very secure corridors, protected by theories, ideologies, books, scriptures, individuals, with no thorns to hurt you and no storms to sweep you off your feet. There will be storms. There will be odd events. So let one be honest at the very first moment. Otherwise there will be hypocrisy. Otherwise enquiry of truth will become an intellectual game and an emotional pastime, a recreation, an additional acquisition, and an additional cerebral acquisition to decorate the prison-house of the 'I'—consciousness. That is happening in the world. People do not realise the seriousness of a religious quest and they hover, they nourish illusions and they live their lives under the pressure of those illusions. You know, it brings tears of blood to the eyes of those who love the human being. What is man doing with himself ? Already he is misusing science and technology. He is doing a lot of damage to himself. But when it is done in the name of religion and spirituality, one does feel concerned.

One has to ask oneself—"do I want it ? Is that the top priority ?" And every discovery implies embracing insecurity.

4

No discovery is made in the prison-house of security; least of all, that of the subtle layers of human consciousness. Consciousness is invisible, intangible For transcending the frontiers of mind you need strength of steel in your nervous system. You need the purity of perception. Otherwise when one is face to face with the contents of the sub-conscious or unconscious, that will sweep off your feet, one can go through a nervous breakdown. One can become neurotic. To deal with the realm of consciousness is a very serious job. It cannot be played around casually. So unless there is the strength to begin the enquiry in full freedom, in the austerity of insecurity, let one not fool around.

Secondly, there may be individuals who have grown into the maturity of egolessness, and who live in the explosive dimension of silence. But if they do live in that dimension, there is no one to assert, to claim to become somebody's master, to get bound in static relationship. There is the incessant, infinite movement of life. So how are you going to claim and how are you going to have relationship? Thus we proceeded to say that enquiry is infinitely moving and so is freedom. There cannot be any static relationship between an enquirer and an enlightened one, relationship in the sense that we know to-day. There can be a meeting, there can be a fusion. there can be a blending for a fraction of a moment and we do not know what a moment is. Perhaps the whole eternity gets condensed in that moment of meeting. And transformation takes place not as somebody's conferring the transformation upon the other. Neither that, nor the other person acquiring that transformation. It is a happening that takes place. It is an event. It is a phenomenon and nothing more.

Those who claim spiritual attainments and achievements know not the beauty of Truth and Reality. Until these points are seen factually as significant points, humanity will not be free of spiritual dogmas and sects. The competitions between the spiritual disciples, their jealousies and the brutalities resulting from those jealousies, envies and competitions are known to us. We are seeing the results of competition as an incentive in economic, political life. That sense of competition, that sense of ownership and acquisition has been transported to the spiritual realm and we have waged many wars on that front.

: 5 :

(Ist March, 1971)

It is an obvious fact for any sensitive and alert citizen of the world that man is not at peace with himself individually and not in harmony with one another collectively. Man suffers from chronic fear and anxiety in his individual life and he suffers from aggression, exploitation and violence in all the fields of his collective activity. Surely this is not the way to live. If there is a friction inside the individual, every minute, every moment of his life, and if whatever he does is either done because of objective compulsion and pressure, or the compulsion of memory from within. if there is an effort which indicates resistance and friction, the person concerned is not living.

To live is to move without pressures and compulsions. To live is to move with the movement of life without friction and resistance of any manner whatsoever. To move in the grace of spontaneity, to move in the relaxation of effortlessness, to move in the elegance of fearlessness, surely that is the content of living. And man has not arrived there. In spite of all the organised religions in the world, man is not capable of living a single moment of his life without resistance, without friction, friction within himself and friction with other fellow human beings. He has not yet discovered the way of love, the way of peace, the way of friendship and co-operation. He needs comparison and competition as the motivation forces for his economic life. He needs acquisitiveness for educating his children.

Hence in spite of all the organised religions in the East as well as in the West, a whole human being, an integrated human being is yet to be born and a human society is yet to come into existence. Not only in the countries of the East, where man is starved, illiterate, in illhealth, has been in slavery for centuries, but even in the European countries as well as United Kingdom, United States of America, man is going through the same miserable plight. There he is living in affluence and yet the psychological poverty, the cultural poverty, the lack of love, the lack of harmony, is so obvious that you cannot miss it. And if a person has to spend half the year, every year in those countries, the inner starvation appears to be as important a problem as the starvation of the body is a problem in the East.

Thus it is very obvious that man has not yet discovered the way of living. That is the challenge. He has not yet discovered the way to live in freedom. Whether we are in the so called democratic countries or we travel through the countries which call themselves socialist, man, the individual is not free, although it may be claimed that the republics of the people are existing. As long as man accepts the authority of society over himself, he accepts the authority of traditional concepts, traditional patterns of behaviour, whether they are moral patterns of behaviour, religious patterns of behavour or political and economic patterns of behaviour, as long as he accepts the authority of patterns of behaviour, he will never be free.

As long as the human animal is addicted to the habit-structure and patterns of physiological and psychological behaviour, handed down to him, transmitted to him, biologically and psychologically, he will not be free. Man has to find out a way of setting himself unconditionally free from all the habit patterns, all the crystallized ways of behaviour, and that is not happening. Not only in educational institutions but also outside them, we allow ourselves to be governed by the ways of behaviour, tests, standards, norms, critreria manufactured for us by those who trade in those areas. We get readymade ideas through books, through magazines. Our entertainment is organized for us Whether it is wireless, the radio, the television, the cinema, entertainment must be organised for us, religion must be organised for us. The states must feed us, the leaders must lead us. We depend from morning till night on being spoon-fed and we feel, we are secure. And when it comes to discovery of truth, first hand personal discovery of the meaning of life, there too we expect to be spoon-fed by someone. When it comes to psychological problems, we want to be spoon-fed, we want to be told, guided, protected by the experts.

We are relegating our responsibility in every field of activity to experts, specialists. We allow our tastes to be regimented and organised and, therefore, man is nowhere free to-day. If you travel in the west, you will see how big businessmen and industrialists have a department of psychology. They appoint psychologists, and specialists to study the trends, the drives, the passions, the demands hidden in the sub-conscious of human beings. How to stimulate those tendencies and how to create a market in the future, is their concern. They have to plan, in advance, for the market and for creating a market for what they are going to produce, they have to study the psychology of men, of women, of children. Look ! To what extent the exploitation goes and I wonder if we realise that ! Specially we in Asia and Africa ! Do we become aware that man is not free from aggression and violence, from dependence and authority, from fear and anxiety ? Do we realise this ? If we do so, we will see that something is missing in the way that man has evolved in the East and in the West, and then we will meet the challenge in an entirely new way. Understanding the nature of challenge, understanding the nature of the problem is half way to its solution. To have a correct perspective of the challenge is to arrive at the solution.

We do get disturbed when we read about the eruption of violence in the Middle East, in Vietnam, in India, Pakistan or between Jordan and Israel and so on. We get disturbed by the symptoms. But are we aware that the malady is much deeper ? It is in the way of living that man has evolved. Something is missing there. Perhaps man has not discovered his own nature; perhaps he has not discovered his totality of being. So a religious enquiry has to begin with what is missing in our way of living. God or Divinity is not outside daily life. The search for God or Divinity cannot take place but in what you call your daily life, your ordinary life, your mundane life. I do not know why the human mind has this curse of fragmentation upon it. What makes man divide life into mundane and spiritual ? What makes him divide it into earthly and divine ? I do not know what is there which is non-divine in this world. Even the minutest molecule of matter is vibrating with energy, which is incalculable. Matter is only the outer crust of the energy contained within. So this curse of fragmentation has got to be purged from the human consciousness; otherwise no religion worth the name will ever evolve.

We have comfortably divided life as worldly and spiritual. No such division exists in reality. This division of life is the soil of all kinds of misery. This fragmentation of life is at the root of all sorrow. Unless we face this fact, I do not think we will be in a position to discover ourselves and to discover the meaning of life. So God is not somewhere away, far away in the sky. I know man has created many concepts of God. He has tried to capture the totality of existence into space and time, into form and shape. He worships that. Let him worship if it helps him to pacify his troubled nerves. But the totality of existence can never be captured exclusively in any one form, whether the form is created by the Hindus or the Buddhists or the Muslims or the Christians.

This curse of fragmentation and division must be seen very clearly. Unless we lay the right foundation we cannot proceed further on the voyage to freedom, to understanding of life, to love, friendship. So, do I see that life is one indivisible whole ? Do I see that everything that I do is either religious in the purest sense of the term, is spiritual in the purest sense of the term or it is not ? Spiritual or religious enquiry is not a mental ectivity to be conducted and carried out in a corner of the house, in a temple, in a mosque, in a monastery, and accepting the authority of traditional economic, political and social concepts and standards for the rest of life. That leads to hypocrisy. I talk of love in the temple and church. I come out and say that I cannot have my business or job without entering into competition and a competitive mind can never love. It will always become callous. I sit in the temple, in the mosque, in the church and talk about love and friendship. I come out and I say in the name of the country or ideology that I am entitled to hate so and so, the communists, the Hindus, the Muslims and so on. This fragmentation and division leads to creation of inconsistent ways of behaviour, and inner contradictions.

Man with capital 'm' to-day has become skizofranic. He talks of love and peace in one breath and prepares for violence and aggression in the next breath. Whether it is the United Nations Organisation or whether it is my planning at home, or whether it is the relationship with my husband, my wife, my children, I am a split personality. And as long as there are incompatible sets of values and contradictory patterns of behaviour that I carry within me, I cannot become a whole human being. To be whole is to be holy and to be divided is to be unholy. That is the sin that man is committing.

Are we prepared to see that this comparative, competitive, acquisitive society with which we are surrounded, in the East and the West, has got to change its way of living ? If we do see, what do we do individually to bring about the necessary change ? The individual is the centre of revolution to-day. Man has tapped the potentiality of organisations and institutions. Now is the age of exploring the potentiality of individual life and it seems to me there is tremendous potentiality in the individual. He can become a living cell of a new current to be set in motion for the whole humanity to see. So how do I set about it ? If and when I have seen how this fragmentation leads to aggression, exploitation and violence, what do I do about it ?

The first thing I do is to observe how I am living to-day. Most of us look into the eyes of other people for recognition, for acceptance, to find out how they evaluate us. I have no source of joy, of a sense of fulfilment, a sense of peace within me. I want to be acknowledged. For the sense of fulfilment, for the joy of living, we depend upon others. That is why I go on comparing myself with other people, not only in material possession but also in psychological, intellectual acquisition, also in religious acquisitions,

I cannot live without looking into the eyes of other people and finding out how they are reacting to my existence, to my behaviour. I am not sure of myself. I depend upon the others. This dependence upon others, this instinct to compare myself with others and to feel fulfilled only when accepted, respected and evaluated by others, seems to be the root of exploitation and violence. Why should not I be happy ? Why should not I be in joy and bliss ? Why should not I feel fulfilled in doing what I see to be right ? Why should not the expression of my inner life give me the sense of fulfilment ? Why should my behaviour be a means to get something back from it. a means to an end ? Going into the causes of the fundamental aggression and violence in human life, is not a pleasant task. But one has to do it. Unless human beings find out a way of feeling fulfilled by the expression of their spontaneity, exploitation and violence will never end. The methods and techniques of aggression, exploitation and violence will become more and more sophisticated. But man will be exploited. So I have to find out why do I depend upon others ? For the joy of sharing, that is quite natural. But a person who is always inhibited by expectation and by the fear of being ignored, cannot share anything with anyone else. Sharing is the activity of free individuals coming together and exchanging spontaneously without expecting anything back from the other person. Sharing can take place only in the state of love, and love knows no fear and love has no expectation.

Love does not want a thing in return—either from human beings or from God, Love feels fulfilled in being. It has no ambition to become something different from what is. And I would like to draw your attention this evening that this urge for becoming something different from what one is, this ignorance of what one factually is, and the temptation to become something else, is the fertile soil for exploitation and violence. That is the soil on which the religious priests stand. That is the soil on which the businessmen, the middlemen between the producer and the consumer stand. That is the soil on which the psychologists. the psychoanalysts and psychiatrists could flourish.

Thus one has to find out a way of having a self-assurance, of having the source of joy and bliss within and a sense of fulfilment in being what one is. That again leads us to the necessity of self-discovery. People feel that when the world is ridden with violence and wars here comes a person talking about self-discovery, as if self-discovery is not related to the elimination of violence from the world. To me, it is basically related to the elimination of exploitation and violence; otherwise I would not have the audacity to take so much time of all of you. So, why do I depend upon others ? Why do I want to look into the eyes of other people and find out whether I am accepted or rejected ? What is this acceptance and rejection ? What is this emotional dependence ? This emotional dependence makes us very cunning. We find out strategy, we go on manoeuvering, manipulating, calculating the reactions of other people, adjusting ourselves to that and binding the other person into the invisible chains of our expectations.

Our relationships to-day are not relationships that could be called humane, full of love. They are only our efforts to adjust to one another's idiosyncrasy, to resist where it is inevitable, to adjust where we can, to hide and suppress what one feels and to show what one does not feel, to try to own and possess others to feel secure. All these efforts are for feeling secured and feeling assured. Now one wonders whether it is possible to get this sense of self-assurance within oneself so that one does not bind other human beings into one's exploitation and fears, and it does seem possible to arrive at such a source of assurance, such a source of security.

First of all, we do not know what joy is. We float on the foam of pleasure and pain. Pleasure is qualitatively different from joy. Pleasure is the reaction of the mind to an agreeable sensation, created by the sense organ coming into contact with some object. Pleasure or pain, these are the sensations and reactions of the mind. Joy is a state of the whole being. It comes into existence in the moment of communion when the mind is not functioning, when one is in the state of egolessness. You stand at the sea-shore, and the beauty of the sea, ocean, the waves, and the light of the Sun on those waves does something to your whole being for a fraction of a second. But then the ego jumps in and says "I would like to have it." How can I have it for a longer time? Will it be possible for me to have it to-morrow? So the mind converts the joy of communion into a sensation of pleasure and wants to own it as an experience and continue it in time. This activity of the mind contaminates the state of communion and you are dragged out of that joy. Joy blossoms in communion, whereas pleasure is a reaction of the mind and we float on the sensations and on the reactions pleasurable and painful.

We try to cling to the pleasurable ones, and avoid the painful ones. So we are not acquainted with joy. Joy that comes, bliss that comes in communion, gives such a sense of fulfilment that one does not have to refer to any other individual and ask for his recognition of that state of assurance. So one has to find out why the mind contaminates the state of communion and reduces the bliss or joy to the mere ashes of pleasure and pain. We are going step by step to find out how individuals become dependent upon one another, and how they prepare the soil for mutual aggression, exploitation and violence.

We do not commit violence with weapons in our daily life, but we throw our anger at one another. We throw the glances full of jealousy, envy, suspicion. These are the weapons that we use from morning till hight. Indifference is a weapon. Suspicion and jealousy—these are the weapons. So why does the mind contaminate the communion, the bliss and reduce it to pleasure or pain ? It seems to me that mind is obsessed with the concept of time. We had seen in one of the talks that man has created concepts and symbols, due to his capacity of self-consciousness, and time is a concept, and time is a symbol that he has created. Reality has no division of days and hours, and minutes and seconds, of weeks and months and years. This currency of concepts created by human beings is mistaken for the reality of life

I do hope you have noticed this that there is nothing like time in reality. There is the day and the night, depending upon the rays of the Sun, in relation to the movement of the earth. That's all. That also is a relative truth, not an absolute one. but psychologically we have created the to-morrow and we have created the yesterday. There is nothing like a yesterday or a to-morrow. There is nothing like continuity in time. As in geometry the supposition of a point which has no magnitude, which has no length, is the foundation on which the whole structure is constructed, in the same way, on the supposition of the present, this moment, we have created the one that is gone before and the one that has to come. And man has forgotten that he created the twenty-four hours constituting a day,

We have been victimised by these concepts and we feel that is the life. So the thought, the idea of future and the desire to continue that sensation of pleasure in time, that is the culprit. Man is haunted by the concept of to morrow. That's why he is afraid even of a simple fact like death, knowing full well that there is birth and there is death. He sees human beings dying every day. He sees the leaves of the tree whithering away in winter and yet he carries the fear of that one small event of death throughout his life. He is haunted by that fear, that creates so many inhibitions in his body and mind, that creates so many distortions and twistings in his relationships, He won't confess it even to himself. So this myth of continuity in time, leading to the fear of to-morrow, fear of future reduces the joy of communion to the sensation of pleasure.

If the mind does not interfere then it would be possible to live in the bliss, in the joy of communion and to respond to it spontaneously, not to want anything in return for that communion, but to allow the communion to take place—the communion with things, the communion with individuals, the communion with challenges of life. It is possible to live in the relaxation of such a communion. It is possible to live in such direct perception of reality, immediate communion with reality and a sponteneous response to it. There will be no time-lag for any friction to take place. There will be no motive to create resistances and there will be no fear of to-morrow to create any expectation.

Only if I could share the beauty of such a bliss, and such a communion; if I could share it verbally with you, I would. But words are such feeble means of communication. They are partial, they are fragmentary. They have become so rigid through centuries, heavily loaded with so many associations that even the simplest word stimulates some religious, moral and spiritual association and the communion between the speaker and the listener becomes very difficult. So, I really do not know how to express that way of living in which communion and bliss or joy lead to a sense of fulfilment every moment, from moment to moment. There is the freshness of that communion, there is the bliss of that joy and spontaneity of an uninhibited response, which is innocence, which is love, which is friendship.

So, to be free of the intervention of mind and to use mind only when the movement of mind is warranted, that seems to be the art or science that we will have to learn. Man has a sophisticated brain. He has found out ways of behaviour, but he has missed the elegance of spontaneity, he has missed the beauty of innocence and spontaneity and we have to rediscover that beauty of innocence and spontaneity to be able to live in joy and bliss so that we don't have to depend upon one another. We don't have to be assured by others. Then we will not be beggars, going around with a begging bowl, expecting recognition from others, respect and prestige from others. We will be able to move without any inhibitions. And one who moves in relaxation as a total human being, moves in love.

This is only introducing a new approach to human problems. This can be correlated with the economic, with the political challenges with which we are confronted to-day. Man is not concerned so much to-day with satisfying decently and scientifically the needs of his body, but he has somehow started worshipping the material things, the comfort, the luxury. We, who are living in a poverty-stricken world, poverty-stricken countries, won't understand the poison that this approach of worshipping the comfort of the body leads to. One has to travel in the affluence-stricken countries to find out where it has led man. We are busy imitating. aping, copying the patterns of industrial revolution, the craze for raising the standard of living, the craze for pleasure, the cult of the body, the cult of sex and so on, we are busy doing that, looking to other countries without realising that their way of living has not enabled them to eliminate violence, eliminate wars, eliminate mental disturbances in individual and family lives, that man is unhappy there.

We are not trying to find out an entirely new way of developing the country economically, industrially. But I would like to point out that competition as a value and profit as an incentive for productive labour, would become unnecessary when a person has a scientific relationship with the needs of his body. He will earn then to satisfy the needs and not out of greed. Then the material possessions would not be an indication of his status and prestige in society. Wrong things have been associated with things that are meant to satisfy the needs of the body.

To look at the body and its needs scientifically, sanely, to provide the needs aesthetically, to provide them scientifically, that is one thing. But the moment you miss the emphasis on a correct perspective, a different malady comes into existence. You must have noticed it in music. The moment the slightest emphasis is increased in ascent or in descent, the whole complexion and the whole quality of the melody changes, its relation to the time of the day goes through a radical change. And that's what is happening to the melody of human life to-day. So, if I am not comparing myself with my neighbour, to find out his reaction to me, if I am fulfilled in satisfying the needs of the body, as I understand them, then comparison and competition as an economic value would whither away, ambition as an economic value would whither away.

I do not know whether you have looked at the problems of to-day in this light. Worshipping, ambition, competition, comparison as an economic value, political value and then talking of love, friendship and peace in individual, spiritual and religious matters is a contradiction in terms. This cannot happen.

If we worship ambition and competition as a value for education, for economic progress, then you can't expect human beings to create a new human society. You cannot have one set of values for economic and political life and another set of values for individual life. If love is a way of living, it will be a way of living in all the fields of activity If friendship and co-operation are worth having. they will be the values in all the fields of activity without an exception and that is what man denies. He does not want to accept. He refuses to believe that love and friendship, co-operation can be of any value. He then refuses to believe that there can be a new technique for bringing about socio-economic or political changes, where anger and jealousy and violence will not have to be used as motivation forces. He refuses to believe there.

He talks of a scientific approach in other fields of activity and when it comes to this, he says "no it can't be, that's human nature", as if we have discovered the totality of human nature. The religious people tell the same thing. They won't allow you freedom. You must have a master, you must have a teacher, you must follow certain ways of behaviour. The so-called revolutionaries come and tell you that you must follow cartain patterns of behaviour—the class-conflict, the class-war, the violence. Or, if you go to the disciples of Gandhi in India, they have their pattern of behaviour. It must be followed.

You and I have to stand up for our own, on our own and refuse to occept any traditional concepts and notions which have anyway failed man and take up the responsibility, shoulder the responsibility of finding out a new incentive, a new way of living.

In the last fifty minutes that I have spoken, I tried to attract your attention to the human problems from an entirely new angle. I said man is nowhere free. He is exploited everywhere. Not only his thoughts and emotions, but his tastes, his hobbies, his entertainment is also exploited. It is organised. Look at the magazines, the advertisements, look at the programme on the televisions, on the radios. How they play on the very subtle passions of man ! How they stimulate ! Even the sex instinct and the sexual urge is exploited. Look at all the advertisements, not only the advertisements of cinemas, but textiles, cosmetics. Turn a page of any magazine, any journal, any newspaper—even the tendermost sexual instinct and urge is exploited for commerce, for trade, for business.

Politicians, businessmen, industrialists, religious priests, capitalists, communists, turn anywhere, the individual is exploited and he allows himself to be exploited in exchange for security· Man wants to be secure at any cost and even after having the illusion of being secure in exchange for the most valuable freedom of his life, he is insecure everywhere. So why not find out if there is an alternative to this way which is ridden with fear, anxiety, aggression and violence. Organised religion and the economic, political institutions of the West right from capitalism to communism have not enabled us to find out that. So what is missing ? Where is the missing link ? There must be something unscientific about our whole way of living.

We can't say that the occidental is superior, or the oriental is superior to the occidental. In all humility we must confess to ourselves that we do not know how to live, to live in harmony, without friction, without resistance, to live in love and spontaneity, and we have to face that challenge. How do we face it ? I find out how do I live and I discover that I live as a beggar right from childhood to the moment when I turn to the grave or the cremation ground. I am a beggar. I have no self-assurance. I have no joy and bliss to give me a sense of fulfilment, in just expressing what I am. But I want to look into the eyes of the other people. The dependence begins. And dependence is the soil in which exploitation and violence breed. We give the ground individually and collectively. Why do we do it? Because we are seeking pleasure.

We have become a pleasure-hunting race and so we miss the beauty of joy. How does one do it? One gets acquainted with the mind, one sees the myth of time that mind has created. Any student of Physics in any University will tell you that there is no continuity in time, there is nothing like succession in life. Life only is. There is a pure isness about life. It can't be divided into yesterdays and to-morrows. This division of time is only a creation of human mind for convenience of collective relationship. This is a symbol and not a reality. So to understand the myth of time and to dehypnotise ourselves of that illusion, of that myth is very necessary and then there is the myth of fragmentation dividing life into individual and collective, political and economic. To purge our minds of that illusion is absolutely necessary. Then only man will, be able to relax and feel fulfilled in getting communed with the moment and what that moment brings to him. Condensed in that moment may be eternity, condensed in that one relationship may be the beauty of love and co-operation.

To be what one is, to express what one is in full freedom; on the mental level, is not possible. I had gone through the whole issue, the psychological issue, in the last three talks given in the G. F. S. Hall. That's why I did not enter into the psychological aspect of total revolution. But on the mental level it is not possible. Mind functions only through time and space, mind functions only through thought and ideas. It cannot function otherwise. So, self-discovery and transcending the limitations of the cerebral organ is absolutely necessary to find out the source of joy within man. When one can look at another person without the desire to beg anything of him, when you can look not only to man, but even towards God without wanting anything in return at all, just for the joy of looking, just for the joy of being there, then in that renunciation, which is the essence of innocence, renunciation which is the content of humillty, then in that renunciation of spontaneity, we can be what we are. WITHIN

The pressures of hypocrisy, the pressures of fear, the pressure of anxiety and worry will drop away completely. Then human beings wiill know what it is to live together. And then there is a hope of creating a new human society, founded on love and friendship. Then only we will understand what compassion means. The content of friendship is compassion. We do not know what it is. We are busy either with self-pity or pitying the others. Whether it is self-pity or pity for others that's the trick of the ego. It is only a vain and proud man who can take pity upon others. Compassion is the flower that blossoms in the soil of humility. So, I said, the challenge of creating a new human society and a new texture of human relationship has got to be faced and for that this adventure of self-discovery, exploring what is beyond the frontiers of mind and brain and growing into the maturity of that dimension is absolutely necessary

As this is the last public talk, perhaps in Colombo, I would like to express my sincere thanks to each one of you who has been kind enough to come and listen to me. Though these talks were not meant for any emotional or intellectual entertainment, so many of you have turned up to listen and I do not take the credit that you have come. It only indicates to me how serious-minded persons do feel concerned about the situation in which man is living to-day. The more the people meet, not in an emotionally disturbed or excited way,—no discovery can take place in the state of excitement, the more obvious is their concern for the state of man.

It has been my humble effort to conduct the meetings and share with you verbally the fundamental issues without creating an atmosphere of excitement, without creating an atmosphere of entertainment, just looking at them with the precision and accuracy of a scientist, stimulating the perception of the challenge, stimulating the formation of the challenge and leaving the rest to individuals themselves, That has been my effort and I am very grateful that so many of you came to participate in these talks.

These talks do not belong to me. No talk worth the name can ever belong to the speaker. One who listens, participates creatively, his contribution to the talk that evolves, blossoms and flowers, is as much important as the verbal expression of the speaker. These talks are the flowers that come into being through the communion of the speaker and listeners. That's why not formally, but from the bottom of my heart, I would like to thank each one of you who has been kind enough to pay attention to these talks and I would like to thank the members of the Reception Committee who took the trouble of inviting me here though none of them had seen me or heard me before. This first visit to Ceylon has overwhelmed me with the kindness and warm hospitality that seems to be characteristic of your land.

Thank you all.

(3rd March, 1971)

I am very glad that it has been possible for us to come together in such a quiet, cool and beautiful place. I would like to point
out that getting together for a couple of days cannot be called a
camp in the true sense of the word. For a camp you need living
together for not less than five days. The participants work together,
cook their meals together, meet in an informal way, not for a for-
mal talk or discussion; but living together in the intimacy of in-
formality, just like the members of a family has its own charm.

The friends who have invited me here did not know what
kind of meetings or getting together have to be arranged and I
have no organisation of my own. So whatever has struck their
imagination, they have very kindly arranged it. We will make the
best use of this opportunity of living together.

In a camp, the first thing for the participants is to observe
silence. Except for discussions about the talks they avoid verbalisation as far as possible. Let it be clear that this is not a camp in
the true sense of the term, This is just getting together for a couple
of days. It must have cost a great deal of labour for the friends
who have organised this.

What are we going to do ? The first thing is to sit in silence
for some time in each meeting. The first thing that occurred to me
when I reached here was how nice it would be if we could be
together without the use of words at all. But we are going to have
another talk and discussion meeting. If you all feel like it we could
sit together for some time in silence in each meeting; just be together without the use of words ! To sit in the relaxed silence of the
physical organism, without making an effort. If relaxation becomes a problem, nothing in the world will help you.

If you sit without any movement in the body, just watch the
behaviour of the body for a few minutes, then you will see that
the bones, the muscles, the nerves, the ligaments of the body are

getting stiff. We have never been educated to ' relax. So sitting quietly becomes a problem. In fact. it is the easiest thing to do. One has to keep the body steady, but not stiff. If steadiness implies stiffness, then within a few minutes the body wants to move. There is pressure in the abdomen, in the spine and so on. So when a person wants to keep the body quiet, the first thing that he notices is lack of education.

There is no obligation, no compulsion at all; but if you don't mind, then we may put our-selves in the state of non-activity; not of inactivity. We know only activity and inactivty. And in inactivity there is either exhaustion or we have a motive for that inactivity; it is purposeful and intentional. Inactivity is an activity of the mind. Not doing with a purpose or motive is another way of doing something. Qualitatively different from the state of doing and not doing, qualitatively different from activity and inactivity is the state of non-activity; i. e. we are not going to convert this state of non-activity into a means to get something back from it. If I sit down and close my eyes in order to get some experience, to see some light, to hear some sounds; that is not non-activity, that is inactivity with a motive.

We do not know how to move without a motive. That is the problem, Now that we are going to sit here, let us not convert this sitting together in silence into a means to achieve something. If it is an ego-centred activity, it will be an inactivity, physical and psychological, but in essence it will be an activity of the ego. Ego has got infinite traps for us and when you are very alert and vigilant to see the strategy of the ego, you will find that it goes on changing its strategy and has infinite varieties of masks and garbs. When you use something to get something as a reward, your mind gets disturbed by pleasure and pain, by success and failure, by activity and inactivity, by likes and dislikes. All this constitutes the diet of the ego.

So we are not going to sit here in silence to get something in exchange for that. Let us try for the fun of it, if we can be in the state of motive-lessness just for a few minutes of the day. If that can be done, then the troubled nerves which have undergone torture in this horrible and unstable economic condition, in this unsteady political situation, get a chance to be soaked in silence, in the state of relaxation. Let the inner organ which has been tortured day and night, relax. Just as when you take a plunge into a swimming pool or a river, you come out refreshed, similarly if you take a plunge into relaxed non-action, it may bring you back refreshed as far as the nervous system is concerned, And if one feels sleepy in that state of non-action, one should not blame oneself. It means that one has not had profound sleep for days together or weeks together and one feels sleepy in the state of non-action. The best thing is to lie down for some time.

It is no use forcing the mind into silence when the exhausted body or the tortured nerves are demanding rest; they are thirsty of that relaxation. The best thing is to lie down and stretch yourself for some time. Even if you sit for a few minutes, those few minutes will have the quality of intensity of half an hour of sluggish and lethargic non-action. It is the quality that matters, it is the intensity of awareness that matters, not minutes or hours.

×   ×   ×

I wonder if you will find it difficult to remember the specific implication of the word meditation which the speaker has in mind throughout our verbal communication. This word meditation does not satisfy me at all for communicating what I would like to communicate. 'Meditation' is derived from the verb to meditate upon something, to contemplate about something. There is a subject and he is indulging in an activity in which there is some object; one has to meditate upon something, some idol, some image. Thus meditation is an activity of the mind; there is an object towards which the activity of the mind is directed. That is the literal meaning of the word meditation in the English language. It has not got pliability and suppleness to indicate something entirely different.

I would like to use the word meditation not as an activity of the mind by focussing its attention on something, but I would like to use this word for a state of being in which mental activity has come to an end, where conscious, sub-conscious and unconscious— all the layers of the mind have ceased to function. In other words, the word meditation for me stands for a state of being where there is no centre as the 'I', the me and no circumference as the 'not me'. Ordinarily, we live at the level where the 'I', the 'me' is the centre and the frontier is constituted by the 'not-me', by the other. Unless we divide life into the 'me' and the 'not-me', the 'I' and the 'other', the ego cannot function. It is the 'other', the 'not-me' that creates duality and in duality the ego goes on functioning in a variety of ways.

So we will have to brush aside the meaning of the word meditation which is deep-rooted in our minds. It is not a mental activity, You may agree with this or you may not agree. Agreement or non-agreement is not the result of coming together. At the end of the meeting you may say that here is a person who speaks nonsense. I am not here to teach or preach anything, but to communicate to you in a very friendly way a very different approach than what is prevalent among the Hindus. Christians, Buddhists etc. Acceptance or rejection, agreement or disagreement is not the point. I do not expect agreement or disagreement on the part of my audiences.

This verbal communication is a friendly exchange. The audience has complete freedom from the first moment. Let them not be under the burden that they have either to agree or not to agree. Unless friends can meet in a motiveless state, living together will have no meaning. Getting together will have no meaning if there are motives of gaining something or giving something.

We are not, at least I am not meeting with any kind of motive at all, except for the joy of being together. And this joy of being together with human beings in different parts of the world is unique. Human beings are the living rays of divinity, behind the masks of I-consciousness, whether they are conscious of it or not. Meeting them is a great joy, at least for me.

Kindly remember that the word meditation for me does not imply any mental activity at all. First of all let us distinguish it from the mental activity of concentration. People sit down, close their eyes and are asked to concentrate upon something. In concentration one has to focus all energy and attention on a Mantra, a picture or an image and sustain that focussing. One has to practise it in 'Hathayoga'. From 'Asana', 'Pranayama' and 'Pratyahara' one comes to 'Dharana', which means to hold, to control. So the focus of energy and attention on a point and sustaining of that focussing through various techniques is the meaning of concentration.

Right from the primary classes, children can be introduced to concentration. It sharpens the mind, it sharpens the brain, it enriches memory, refines receptivity, increases the power of retention i. e. the mind becomes very powerful, very sharp. The latent powers of the mind manifest themselves, Thus concentration is a very useful activity as far as cultivation of the powers of the mind is concerned. I wonder if you have read the life of Vivekananda, one of the great sons of India, who could read 300 to 400 pages of a book in one hour and tell you what was written on what page, not the summary, but the whole of it.

Concentration has nothing to do with meditation. It is the cultivation and development of the powers hidden in the mind. Those who practise concentration, they attain the power of clairvoyance. Time and space are the limitations of the mind. When one goes beyond the limitations, psychic powers like clairvoyance, clairaudience, reading the thoughts of other people before they are verbalised,—are attained. They imply the functioning of the 'I'—consciousness on a very subtle plane and it is not without danger to cultivate and develop these powers.

If the body has not been purified by a scientific way of living, by scientific diet, by scientific relationship with sleep, cultivation of psychic powers can be full of danger. In human life purity is the only strength required for discovering what truth is. By purity I imply a scientific relationship with the body and the mind; it has not got any ethical or moral odour as far as I am concerned. Through a scientific approach to the needs of the body, by providing for them in a decent way, in an aesthetic and artistic way, one arrives at a certain strength. If that strength is not developed in the physical and psychological organism, encounter with the latent powers of the psyche, encounter with the occult world later on can cause a nervous breakdown, it can shatter a person.

Thus cultivating this power of concentration is a mental activity. It is not meditation, it has nothing to do with meditation. I can sit down and concentrate for some time, but the 'I', the 'me', the ego cannot meditate. Meditation is not an activity to be indulged in by the 'I'—consciousness. The sense in which the word has been used in the East and the West implies that it is an activity of the mind. 'I was meditating.' How could the 'I' meditate ? It simply means that the person was sitting in silence or was concentrating.

Let us remove this illusion from our minds that concentration and meditation are one and the same thing. Concentration is not meditation. This is the first thing to observe. As one develops the powers of the psyche, one gets visions and experiences of all that is contained in the sub-conscious. This has nothing to do with meditation. Meditation. in essence, is a state where total mental activity comes to an end. Experience is not possible in meditation. In experience, at the centre of the consciousness there is the experiencer i. e. there is the 'I', the 'me', the ego to get experiences. They may be transcendental, trans-sensual or non-sensual, but all the time they are experiences.

Experience is an event in which you identify and recognise. Recognition is possible only when you refer the event to something known. We refer the event to somenting that has taken place in the past, compare it with that. Then only you can identify. Every identification and recognition has its root in the known, in the past i. e. the 'I'—consciousness is at the centre. The 'I'—consciousness converts an event into an experience by identifying it with the known. It is a very complex activity. People feel very happy when they get some visions and experiences. They feel that they are very religious, that they are making much progress. Actually, this is only playing around with the sub-conscious. There is nothing religious about it, leave alone the word spiritual.

So when you go on practising concentration, some psychic powers are developed and after their development premonition, precognition etc. start coming to the conscious level. Experiences of the whole human race are contained in our consciousness. They find their way to come up to the uppermost level which is now quiet. So having experiences is not a religious activity at all. Experience-mongering is not spirituality; it is not the content of religion. Of course, this is not a very pleasant thing to hear.

We have not got the freedom to look at what we have read or heard; to read or listen with humility. We acquire it and we think it is our own. We lack the susceptibility to look at something with an enquiring mind. As soon as you intellectually acquire an idea, it becomes your possession, you identify yourself with that acquired idea, acquired theory, you get a kind of vested interest in it. If one listens to a talk or reads a book to acquire, to add to one's psychological possession, one does not learn from it, one does not live it, you do not digest it and undigested, acquired knowledge and experience creates so many perversions, so many morbidities. It has its own malady that results from psychological possession.

After the practice of concentration, when visions and experiences come up, one feels superior to others. There is a charm about that person. There is a kind of intoxication about him, something unusual about him. People are attracted towards him and the enquirer is lost in his own charm at that stage. That is why I said it is a slippery ground. If one does not get attached to these powers, if one does not get attached to this event, then one goes through it. Events are bound to take place inside just as they take place outside. Visions, hearing of sounds—all this will happen because inside also there is a world; the five elements are working there too.

So many things will happen when you practise Yoga for physical health. When you practise Yoga for the development of the mental powers, many events will take place. Then you want to find out their interpretation, you refer to books, want to analyse them. So the state of observation, the state of enquiry ends. Analysis, interpretation, attachment to the events—all these come up and the 'I' consciousness begins functioning on a very subtle plane. To become aware of the working of the ego on the physical plane is comparatively easy, but to be aware of the tricks of the ego on the psychic plane is very difficult. One moment of inattention and you are already in the trap. One moment of distraction, one moment of attachment and the snare of the ego is there. Attachment results in inattention, indulgence results in inattention. And renunciation and indulgence are obverse and converse of the same activity. They are both mental activities or activities of the ego. 'I renounce' this is the working of the ego, the working of the 'I'.

Anything that is intentionally undertaken by the I-consciousness as an activity is not meditation. Let us clear the ground in this first meeting and let us find out what is not meditation. Even the experiences and visions which are inexplicable do not constitute meditation, Remember that as long as there is experience, the 'I', the 'me' is functioning. It is not a state of meditation. Only when all the experiences subside, only when the ego goes into abeyance, does one enter the area or the field of silence; not until then. Let us not mistake concentration, the psychic powers developed through concentration and the occult and transcendental experiences for meditation, for a spiritual quest.

Let us see very clearly that they are the activities of the mind, they are in the realm of the psyche. Concentration is not meditation. To force the mind with any method or technique is not meditation. In fact, there cannot be any technique, any method, any path. It is the pathless path. Meditation is something unrelated to time and space. Concentration is practised in time. Wherever there is time, there is space. They go together. In fact, time and space are not different. Meditation is the state of being unrelated to time and space. Obviously, there cannot be a way, a method or a technique.

There is no 'how to meditate'. Love is a total state. It expresses itself because it has its own dynamism. If someone asks me how to love, there cannot be an answer. There is a 'know-how' about physical and intellectual matters. But there is no 'know-how' to love and no 'know-how' to understanding. One cannot know how to meditate. It is a question of total state.

It will thus be clear that one cannot meditate. It is not a mental activity. To see this as a fact one has to experiment with concentration and see what happens. One has also to experiment with a state where the mind functions not. where the ego operates not, in order to find out whether the two are different. Then only one will see the difference as fact and not as an idea gathered from somebody's talk or book. If it is an idea, it will complicate matters. So you will see that meditation is not a mental activity through which one gets marvellous, extra-ordinary experiences.

Through meditation one is not going to achieve or attain freedom or liberation. Freedom is not something to be attained or achieved. And religion for us is the means of attaining something, attaining God, attaining liberation. All this is mental activity; only the sphere or field of activity is changed, the object is changed. For us all these activities like meditation, understanding, attending talks, joining camps etc. are actuated by ambition. Ambition takes us there. The ego wants to acquire something. So we go to these gatherings, attend talks, participate in camps, read books for acquiring something. From the physical and material objects the ego turns to the extra-sensory, non-sensual objects. The ambition of acquiring is the motive behind reading books or listening to talks. Thus the very source of enquiry is contaminated by ambition, by motive.

In fact, there is nothing to acquire, attain or achieve in religion. One has to understand and live in that understanding, not to acquire, own, possess and show off. But for us even divinity is to be acquired, freedom is to be acquired. Whether one says 'I am the body, I am the mind' or he says 'I am Brahman', what is the difference ? The 'I'—consciousness is there all-right. The consciousess that I am Brahman is again a very subtle kind of bondage. So there is nothing that can be attained. It is a total growth into a new dimension of consciousness and living and moving out of that. It is the question of growing into the maturity of understanding.

Thus first of all, meditation is not a mental activity and secondly there is nothing to attain in reality. That is the test of real enquiry. If I am enquiring to attain, to achieve, to acquire, then the enquiry is contaminated by ambition and ambition creates its own pressures and tensions. It pollutes the enquiry, it colours the perception. So one has to ask oneself why am I interested in finding out what meditation is, what freedom is, what Truth is ? This question is very fundamental. If the momentum of enquiry gets extinguished, if it subsides when you see for yourself that there is nothing to acquire in religion, then the enquiry is not real. Freedom cannot be acquired, one can live in freedom, but it cannot be imprisoned in the 'I' consciousness and owned or possessed. Illumination cannot be and is not the experience of the mind. One has to see whether the momentum of enquiry subsides or remains unabated, when there is no room for the play of the ambition of acquiring; attaining, owning possessing, experiencing.

Enquiry is not a game of children; it is not to be played around. How many will be interested in self-discovery, in finding out what the ultimate reality called God is, if they know that they, holding a body, a psychological structure, cannot own that freedom and cannot carve something out of it. And who knows, they as separate entities or identities may be completely melted. The ego, the 'I' the 'me' may be completly eliminated, who knows ? Discovery of what Truth is, what God is, what the Reality of life is, is not full of security. Everything is not very smooth there. There are no blueprints. To let the total mental activity cease to function, to let the ego go into abeyance and to be with the unknown is not a game of security. It needs a kind of fearlessness to come face to face with that which is not mapped out. which has no path. An enquirer going within and taking a voyage into himself makes his own path. It is a voyage within, not without. So nobody will be able to create the path for him, nobody will be able to take his hand, hold his hand and take him through.

It is a voyage to be taken alone to discover the nature of bondage, to understand the nature of bondage and through that understanding to transcend bondage altogether. So the third point is that not only there is nothing to acquire, but the inner voyage has to be taken alone. No husband can help the wife nor wife the husband. They may be living under the same roof, they may be eating at the same table, but the inner voyage has to be taken alone, if one is willing to be alone, The loneliness that we know and go through is not aloneness. There is a difference between loneliness and aloneness.

When I want company and miss something in its absence, I am lonely. I am looking forward to have somebody with me. The need for company and lack of company constitutes loneliness. When I am compelled to be with myself, not looking at someone, not expecting someone to be with me and am happy with myself, then there is solitude, then there is aloneness. You are not alone when you go to a cave. You carry all your expectations, jealousies, envies with you. To be alone in a cave or in society is an entirely different thing. Solitude is à state of aloneness, solitude is not isolation or going away from the people or going away from the home. I do not know if I am making the difference between loneliness or isolation and aloneness or solitude, sufficiently clear. In isolation and loneliness there is fear. In solitude there is a relaxation of fearlessness. In aloneness there is a sense of fulfilment and happiness of being with oneself. So this is a voyage to be taken in aloneness. If we are afraid of taking it alone, then I think, we need not venture upon meditation. This is living in the realm of the unknown, in the solitude of understanding.

Knowledge can be a collective activity, but meditation is the perfume of individual communion with life, It is not a collective activity. If you take a book and read it together collectively, you can gather knowledge from it. as we do in schools and colleges. We gather, collect and acquire information collectively. So knowledge and information can be collective activity, but understanding is the perfume of individual communion with reality. That is why I say that it is a voyage to be taken in the solitude of aloneness.

If and when one has seen all these points as facts, then one can proceed to let the mind alone. The mind cannot be of any use in meditation which is not a mental activity. We have to let the mind alone, not fight against it. You can say that we let the mind alone but the mind does not let us alone; it starts wandering and chattering as soon as we sit quiet. What can we do about it ? Nothing is to be done against it or with it. Just watch its wanderings, just as you watch the tide, the clouds or the flowers Find out the frequency of its wandering in different directions. The moment you start watching, please do not resist the wandering or chattering of the mind. The moment you start resisting, you will dissipate your energy. The mind which is chattering and wandering has the momentum of all the feelings, all the thoughts and emotions contained in the unconscious and sub-conscious. The wandering of the mind has tremendous momentum. Your biological inheritance, psychological inheritance, they are all there, You cannot fight against this momentum of millions of years with your acquired strength of 30, 40, 50 years. Man has tried that, it does not work.

Suppression and denial have been tried and experimented in all the religions the world over. You suppress the mind at one point and it has an upsurge at another point. Suppression does not work, it does not pay. What did Siddhartha, the son of Suddhodana arrive at after 48 days of fasting, when he accepted 'Payasa' from Sujata ? He arrived at 'Madhyama-marga' or the golden mean and the four noble truths, as you call them. So fighting against the momentum of the mind is not warranted.

As opposed to suppression and denial, indulgence has been tried in the occident. Satisfy every demand of the mind and the body. Satisfy all the impetuous demands, do not deny anything to the body and the mind. This has also been tried. Does it work ? A sane and peaceful way of life has not been arrived at as yet. So let us observe the wandering and chattering of the mind without analysing, interpreting.

We saw how concentration is a mental activity in time and space; it is an ego-centred activity. Meditation is not a mental activity at all. It is a state where total mental activity comes to an end. Concentration develops certain powers. Man wants some kind of powers in order to have the sense of owning. Concentration is useful in the realm of mental activity, but there is nothing religious about it.

The cessation of total mental activity does not take place if the person is ignorant about the mind; if he has not acquainted himself with the mechanism of the mind. You cannot dodge the mind. So one has to get acquainted with the mind and its way of operation. How does one get acquainted ? One has to get acquainted with the restlessness of the body and the mind. Instead of resisting the momentum of the mind, start watching. Man has not been educated to watch. He has to learn to watch and start watching for the fraction of a second. The alertness of watching will be lost again and again, but the moment one is aware of the inattention, one comes back to attention, Learning how to observe is the beginning. It is a voyage to be taken inwards, to be taken in the solitude of aloneness. These are the basic points that we saw today.

: 7 :

(5th March, 1971)

It is a joy to speak to the younger generation about some of the fundamental issues that the youth in Asia and Africa is facing to day. I do not know what subject is going to interest the other people. But the hope of the world is only with the young people, the students of Universities who have not yet developed vested interest in economic or political theories, in religious or cultural theories, who have not identified themselves or committed themselves to any rigid traditional patterns of behaviour. There is no hope of revolution from any other class of society including the labour class, the trade unions, the workers etc. This is not being said in order to flatter the younger generation, but it is a simple fact. The mind of the worker class has been bourgeoised, it has become as bourgeois, as money-minded as the capitalists or the governments of socialist countries where the means and instruments of production have been nationalised. Thus individuals or groups of individuals have become money-minded everywhere, and those who evaluate everything in terms of money, can never bring about a revolution. Whether in Asia, Africa, Europe or U.S.A., as far as I can see, the hope is with the youth. The youth is the hope or despair of to-morrow. So I thought that as I meet the younger brothers and sisters of India or elsewhere, so I would talk informally to young friends in Ceylon.

Those who want to understand the challenge with which humanity is faced to-day, will have to study very closely the thought of Marx, Mao and Gandhi. To my mind, we are living not only in post-Marxian or post-Maoian era, but also in post-Gandhian era and we will have to look at them. No one can ignore the contribution of these very great celebrities. When I speak of Marx, I do not imply any political or econmic alignment. I am not a politician or economist, but a lover of humanity cannot afford to neglect the contribution of these great men. As you cannot ignore the advances in science and technology, similarly you cannot ignore them.

When in 1842, the book of Karl Marx was published, it created a great stir. One can visualise the greatness and the nobility as great as that of Lord Buddha that must have caused him to say that poverty is man-made, not made by God and man can undo what he has done. He gave an entirely new interpretation to the whole of human history. I will not go into the details of the material interpretation of history and into the propriety or otherwise of that interpretation, but I am just indicating an entirely new approach to the whole human history.

Marx said that poverty can be undone, economic exploitation is man-made and it can be eliminated from the face of the whole globe; that state-boundaries have been created by vested political interest and they can be eliminated. Just to visualise, to have the vision to say that workers of the whole world can unite and eliminate their exploitation. A classless society, a stateless globe and an exploitation-less human relationship, what a vision ! To speak of that vision ! You cannot imagine to-day how it must have enthused the hearts of people, whether they were in old bodies or young bodies. Sometimes vibrations of youth do not saturate the young body, they do the old body.

The dialectical materialism, the material interpretation of history, the theory of classes, the vision of elimination of classes, —one has to look at it as one has to look at the industrial revolution in order to understand the economic structure existing in democratic, socialist and communist countries. One has to understand the teachings of Marx, Mao and Gandhi in order to appreciate the cry of the younger generation, in order to get at its roots. Let us find out the foundation, wherein lie the roots of this cry and make a critical study. The youth of to-day is very critical about religion, very critical about all discipline, moral or social and I do not blame them. But when it comes to economic theories, somehow the critical approach slips into the background.

After the industrial revolution, urbanisation i.e. taking the agrarian population to the cities for working in the factories, workshops, centralisation of units of production—all that was considered necessary, because it was said that the farmer was very orthodox and was not capable of bringing about a revolution. Marx wanted to create a Proletariate class. They would unite and work together. His idea was that the nature of exploitation will be highlighted by the creation of that class, the inner conflict and the nature of exploitation will come to the focus of their attention. He wanted to create a Proletariate class where trade unions and labour unions could be organised, where the worker, the labourer could be organised. He held that they should be organised in cities and towns, because the farmer in the agrarian sector does not realise the nature of exploitation. In this connection one will have to take into consideration the socio-economic and political context of the whole of Europe.

I wonder if you have noticed the history of the Bolshevik revolution, the first attempt in 1905, how it failed, the second attempt in 1912 and its failure, the rift between the Bolsheviks and Mensheviks, and the third attempt in 1917, the October revolution and its success. It is very illuminating and thought-provoking to study the causes of the rift, the failure and success of that revolution. It is not worthwhile to talk about Marxism, Leninism, communism etc. without studying all this.

In the revolutions drawing inspiration from Marx personal jealousies, personal envies were used as motivation forces. In order to create a class-mind, a proletarian mind, jealousy, hatred, anger—all these have been elevated to the level of motivation forces for revolution and have been used as such. Not that the revolutionaries were thirsty for blood-war. This is the class of exploiters, this is the class of the exploited—this class-consciousness was created for bringing about a change in the socio-economic structure. I am proceeding vary slowly, but only an outline of the thought of these three great men can be given here. I am not here to give a talk on the history of revolutions in the world, industrial revolution, the development of the technique of revolution, how humanity turned from the violent to the non-violent revolution i. e. the development of thought about revolution in Europe, England, Asia etc. Now, we have to remember how the personal instincts incorporated in the human structure have been elevated to the level of motivation forces for revolution.

In studying the history of the Chinese revolution one has to
6

see the history of the great march from South to North; one has to study the role of Mao-tse-tung, Chou-en-lie and their associates, the other Chinese leaders. One has to study the tradition of Chinese culture, thoughts of Laotse and Confucius and others, That is very important. Mao refused to believe that the farmer in the agrarian sector cannot bring about a socio-economic revolution. It is one step forward. Marx said that the agrarian sector cannot become Proletariate, the farmer cannot have the vigour and enthusiasm necessary for revolution If you study Mao, you will see that the march from the South to the North has a very romantic history; it is a very thrilling epic of human development. The socio-economic and political change in China has been brought about by organising the farmer, the cultivator in the village. The role of the villagers in China in bringing about the ultimate success in 1949, the austerities, the suffering, the privations that the revolutionaries had to undergo—all this constitutes a very interesting part of human history.

Here you find an absolutely new trend relevant to the context of Asia and Africa, where people live in the villages. If mobilisation of the farmer is not possible, no socio-economic change can be brought about in Asia and Africa. Not to impose authority upon the farmer, not to whip him around with a group or party, but to mobilise his labour, initiative, energy for revolution. I wonder if you have looked at this aspect of the Chinese revolution. It is a cultural contribution of Mao and his colleagues to the technique of revolution. In the last 25 years the Indian Government has been planning for industrialisation of the country, without mobilisation of the energy of the farmer. I do hope that a new pattern of industrial revolution will be discovered, where the villager will not have to run away from the land. It should not be impossible to apply science and technology to small units of production distributed all over the country. A new approach to the pattern of industrial revolution will be discovered by the Indian young people.

Russia and other socialist countries have copied the pattern of the industrial revolution of Europe. They have adopted centralised economy and centralised business Wherever there is centralisation of economic power, political power is bound to be centralised. You cannot escape that. And then military power is also centralised. Wherever there is centralisation of economic power, political power, and military power, all talk of freedom of the individual is meaningless, they are all dead words. Wherever there is centralisation of these three powers, there is bound to be exploitation. Even if centralised economy is based on socialism and is set up after a revolution, a new beaurocracy will come into existence. This has been realised by persons like Jillas in Yugoslavia. Mobilisation of the initiative of the farmer and bringing about a revolution, a socio-economic and political change through the farmer involves taking a new path. In creating this new path in China, anger, hatred, jealousy, violence—all these were employed in the agrarian society. Violence is the last sanction for the revolutionaries, it is the last sanction for states, it is the last sanction in international relations; even for the United Nations Organisation it is the last sanction. As long as violence is the last sanction, as long as it has authenticity and cultural value, no real revolution is possible. Violence has no authenticity as far as private relations are concerned, but when it comes to an ideology, a nation, a country, the same hatred violence against human beings becomes something noble. This inner contradiction of human nature has got to be resolved. It is a challenge to the constructive and creative energy of the younger generation to discover a technique for bringing about a socio-economic and political change without employing destructive forces like anger, jealousy, hatred as motivation forces.

You must have read in the newspapers how so many people have been killed in Dacca. In India you cannot look at a newspaper without reading that so many were stabbed in streets or shot down by the police or army. Organised violence and unorganised violence—, this is the greatest challenge to the decency and spiritual force of human beings. Exploitation, violence, bloodshed are rampant to-day. Talking of non-violence and working with violence will not help. The Indians have tried that. For collective action you do not have to shed the blood of human beings. It is no use saying that there cannot be another way, because that has been the way for thousands of years and that it has got to be the same for all times.

You and I have to refuse to believe that it is impossible to find out an alternative, we have to take up the challenge. The young people in America are doing it; they are opposing the U.S. policy in Vietnam. Just imagine two hundred thousand young men and women gathering in New York against the Vietnam Policy or against the law of segregation. The younger generation in America is stimulated to the depth of their being, because the killing in Vietnam has become a problem of life and death for the young boys and girls, not only because they want to escape from the killing itself, but also because of the unkind view behind all that. They are disillusioned and have a sense of revolt against violence. Human civilisation and culture have no role to play if they cannot find out an alternative to killing human beings for solving the problems of law and order at home and for meeting communal tensions. So I think that is the basic challenge The youth in Asia and Africa have to take up the challenge and see if an alternative can be found out. I think that is the basic problem for the young men and women in Asia and Africa.

In the technique of Mao and Chou-en-lie one feels glad at heart that the farmer, the rural population was not condemned. They were considered worthwhile and their energies were harnessed. Not only that, they conducted another experiement in 1956, which unfortunately failed. This experiment was related to efforts to decentralise the indusrialisation and the economic sector and power. Why it failed and how it failed is not to be considered here; though it is a very interesting question. How they began with enthusiasm in the workshop and in the commune and how and why they failed is a separate question. But their effort and this experiment in decentralising industry was also a turning point in history.

Now let me go to India. In 1915 Gandhi returned to India from South Africa. He wanted to liberate India. You will find that a few more persons were coming up with that aim. Gandhi said, "we are unarmed people, now the difficulty of being unarmed is to be converted into an opportunity." A revolutionary is he who likes to be an artist of life; otherwise he cannot bring about a revolution. He said—"We are unarmed people, millions and millions of us; how can we convert this difficulty into an opportunity for bringing about liberation ?" energies of all people were harnessed—rural and urban population, literate and illiterate people, men and women, young and old, rich and poor—all were brought together. Not only people of the middle classes, not only the farmers, but people of all classes joined hands. And thus the struggle for independence became the struggle of the people of India.

All political leaders who came before Gandhi used to laugh. They used to say—what are women going to do there ? What are children going to do there ? It is also a very romantic story. Thus Gandhi went a step further; not because he wanted to worship non-violence (that came later on). He also employed the religious and cultural instinct, but the technique of converting a difficulty into an opportunity was the main point. We will have to find out what are the difficulties of the people and how they can be skilfully converted into an opportunity to extract their constructive energy.

Not out of helplessnes, not out of anger, bitterness and jealousy, but out of a kind of artistic skill, Gandhi employed the technique of non-violence in the struggle for independence. And that was a sweep of his genius, I must say. Slavery of a thousand years, not only 150 years of British rule, accepting destiny, fatalism, all this had to be encountered by him. What amount of work he must have done !

The thing that he said was that on the one hand you have to fight and eliminate the British rule and on the other hand you have to lay the foundation of a new economy right from now. Nobody in India could understand his insistence on the spinning wheel, nobody could understand the emphasis on self-employment for the villager, the farmer. No one could understand the labour-intensive economic planning that he wanted to bring about, no one could understand his insistence on avoiding capital-intensive planning. He did not want to convert India into a beggar country. 550 million people are beggars today. Ours is a community of beggars, as we have not realised the inherent strength of human labour and animal labour at our disposal. Gandhi had realised that and as a consequence he launched upon the programme of the elimination of caste system, the use of spinning wheel, sitting down in prayers etc. He had faith in God, he had faith in the innate goodness of the human heart. Others had not.

Respect for individual freedon and initiative is the basis of democracy. If you do not have faith in tne innate goodness of man, it is no use giving him the right to vote. In this way we will have democracy only in paper.   (Incomplete)

: 8 :

(7th March, 1971)

As you might have noticed, I have come to your land of Shri Lanka not for preaching or teaching anything, but have come in a very friendly way to communicate my observation as well as my understanding of life, not to propagate anything, not to convert the people of Shri Lanka to any specific approach or attitude to life but in the simple spirit of sharing.

There cannot be a new truth. Truth is eternal. Truth is the same. But the beauty of personal discovery is unique with every individual, whether it be a Vinoba, a Krishnamurty or any X, Y Z. Personal discovery of truth is for living and not for preaching or teaching. So, when a person discovers it first hand and lives it in every field of his activity, then there is a unique beauty about the expression of that living truth. It is true that I have been in close contact with Vinobaji. It is true that I have known Krishnamurti, I could not say very closely, and I have tried to study the teachings of these two great human beings who were born in India, but who belong to the whole humanity. But I am not here to speak about them to you.

I was wondering how you react, respond to the situation—political, economic, cultural, religious, not only in Ceylon, in India,—in Asia, but all over the world. I wonder if you have noticed that man is not living in peace individually, and not in love and harmony collectively. He has inhabited the globe for millions of years and yet in the East as well as in the West he has not found out a way to live with one another in love and harmony, in friendship and co-operation. There might have been individuals in the East and in the West who discovered the source of eternal joy and bliss and were able to radiate the light of that bliss and the light of that love through their words, through their behaviour, but collectively we have not found a way. We have not found a way of living as human beings, whether we refer to the economic life, or we refer to the social or political life. Our economic structures are based on competition, They are based on profit motive. They are based on conflict of interest among the people of one community. Politically we have not found out a way of administering or managing the human relationship with the consent of the people, respecting their freedom, respecting the individual initiative, having faith in the innate goodness of man.

We may talk about very many things—metaphysical theories, high flown talk about philosophy, psychology; the e are so many religions, thousands of mosques, temples, churches, monasteries and Ashrams and yet man has to discover the fountain of love and joy within himself so that the extension of his behaviour, the relationship with others would not lead to competition, comparison, aggression, exploitation and violence.

We are living in the age of violence. Our consciousness flutters with ambition, exploitation, aggression and violence. At home, the aggression and violence may be expressed in harsh words, criticism, contempt, the husband suppressing the wife or the children, or the wife dominating over the husband. It may be expressed through glances, through gesticulation, through words, using indifference as a weapon, sometimes using anger as a weapon, sometimes using expectation as a network to bind others, There are very subtle ways of exploiting others or dominating over others. In family relationship also if we watch our behaviour from morning till night, we may not find the glow of love, love that does not depend and that does not expect, that finds fulfilment in expressing, unfolding its own content, its own existence, So what we call family relationship between a man and a woman, husband and wife, their children, that also has not got the freshness of dynamism of love and peace.

We may talk about religions when we are within the walls of a temple, or a mosque or a church. We may talk about the Omnipresent, Omniscient, Omnipotent God and even worship, carry out some rituals, chant the Mantra. The moment we are out of the temple, we have the untouchables and touchables. then we have one code of conduct for our superiors in caste, in money, in power and so on. We may say God permeates tbe whole world while we are sitting in a religious gathering and the moment we step out of the doors, the whole behaviour, the whole attitude, the whole approach changes.

It is a kind of split personality, my dear friends, that the same man is living through affectionate and gentle worship in a temple, but when he goes to office, when he goes to business, he accepts the authority of worn-out, traditional economic concepts. He accepts profit motive as an incentive for productive labour. He accepts the theories right from Malthus to the latest economist whosoever he be, and he becomes a victim of those traditions and concepts. As a political member he accepts the theories of the 18th or the 19th century, accepts the authority of the concept of the state, national sovereignty, and so on, and then hatred and anger and jealousy becomes sanctified in the name of ideologies, in the name of patriotism, in the name of nationalism. Whether we refer to the so-called democratic countries or we refer to the socialist countries, this acceptance of the incompatible sets of values and contradictory codes and ways of behaviour has become the way of life we are living in the East as well as in the West and it seems to me that there is a crisis in the human psyche. Unless the human being finds out a way of resolving his inner contradiction of accepting incompatible sets of values for different categories and different fields of activities, unless he resolves the inner contradiction and conflict in his own being of accepting competition as a value in one field of activity and co-operation as a value in another field of activity, talking of love in the field of religion, spirituality, philosophy and sanctifying anger, hatred, jealousy, violence in another field of activity, man will never be happy. He will never be able to live as a human being.

So though it may be found arrogant and presumptuous on my part, the first point I would like to make to-day is that man has not yet discovered his own being. He has not discovered his own roots. He is an uprooted animal. He does not know where the source of his life comes from. He does not know the fountain of joy and bliss within him. That is why a religious or a spiritual quest becomes one of the musts of to-day, not academically, not theoretically, but as a problem of life and death. We will have to find out what it is to live. What is love ? What is happiness ? And why is it that our lives are ridden with, cluttered with so much violence, so much bitterness, so much exploitation, mutual and reciprocal aggrandisement ? We will have to discover this for ourselves, find it out.

Personal discovery of truth is the essence of religion. Whether we read a book, a scripture. ˙whether we listen to a saint, a Yogi, a teacher, whether we listen or whether we read; the primary responsibility of a human being is to find out the validity of what he has read, and what he has listened to. If he accepts without finding out the validity thereof, without discovering the content of what he has read; if he accepts that, then that blind acceptance and that sheepish following or conformity does not contribute any life to him personally or to the society he lives in.

Religion is a dynamic force. If there is really one religious person, he will become a living cell for a total revolution in the society that he moves in. So, it is not borrowing things, it is not trying to grasp ideas and theories intellectually and store them in memory. It is not that which will make you religious. But as soon as one hears a thing, to find out if it is valid, to find it out and discover it in one's daily relationship is the essence of religion. We do not need believers and disbelievers. We need individuals of faith. Once you discover the meaning, the truth, the reality, then it becomes the essence of your life. Then faith in that which you have discovered, becomes the substance of your whole living. Nobody can deprive you of that; not even death.

We have to find out why man is not at peace with himself, in harmony with his body and mind. Why does he live under so many stresses and strains ? Why is he so restless ? Why is he like a tender leaf tossed about by feelings and thoughts, every moment troubled and tortured by contradictory ambitions, drives and passions ? Why he be tortured individually and why is he not in love and harmony with other human beings ? So the whole challenge, the crisis in the human psyche boils down to these aspects of the same problem.

Why am I not in harmony with the body and the mind ? Why do I have to use the whip of some rules and regulations for the body, whether it comes to my relationship with diet, food, taking physical exercises, my hours of sleep, my relationship with clothes, things that I use ? Why do I have to use certain incentives either telling the body that it will have some reward if it behaves in one way, or it will be punished if it does not behave in that way ? Why do I have to use the positive and negative incentives ? But fear or temptation has the incentive for correct behaviour because without incentive of fear or temptation we do not move from morning till night. Somebody has got to tell me that if you behave in this way, you will get this as a reward, in this life or the next life, or, you will be punished here in this life or after you die.

Why this fear and temptation ? May be because we have never looked at the physical organism in love and tenderness, care and concern, a first hand acquaintance with the biological orga- nism that has been given unto us, the most beautiful; the most sophisticated and refined instrument, infinitely more sensitive than any of your stringed instruments like Sitar, or a Vichitra-Veena, or a violin. So, first hand acquaintance with the biological orga- nism, friendship with the body, a kind of respect and affection for the physical organism, seems to be vitally necessary.

We either fondle the body, indulge in the blind demands of the body or we suppress it, repress it and go on denying and negat- ing the demands. Indulgence and suppression or denial, these are obverse and converse of the same weakness. So, without entering into worshipping the body or denying and condemning it, can we simply look at it ? The muscular, the glandular, the nervous system, the neurons, the tendons, the blood circulation, the beauty of inhaling a breath, retaining it and exhaling it like a rhythm in a melody ! The getting up, the sitting down, the moving about, all this beautiful human organism, can we look at it ? Feeding it after understanding the demands, necessity, and not feeding it out of certain traditions or out of certain tread and tracing, not treating the body as a victim of patterns of behaviour, as a victim of ways of behaviour, crystallised into our family, into our community, into our country. But looking at it, what does it need ?

The limitations of biological inheritance, the psychological inheritance, idiosyncrasies, studying them, and so arriving at a correct and scientific diet or relationship of food, which does not make a farce out of it, either way, positively or negatively. A sensitive approach to diet so that the body is neither over-fed nor under-fed, not worshipped and indulged in and not tortured in the name of austerity. Arriving at it so that it does not become a problem to be verbalised, to be ruminated about, finding out the way of keeping the body in health, supple, pliable, always sharp, always fresh. The tremendous power that this human body has !! We have not even tapped it.

We do not use all the powers of the muscular and the glandular system. Fortunately for the orient there have been the science and art of Yoga, which have developed systematically from 553 B. C. when Patanjali codified the Yogasūtra. We have had this. We talk about it. But how many of us study and apply what we have studied to our daily life, to carry the human body in its grandeur, dignity and beauty ? Why should it be over-tired ? Why should it be over-fed ? Because we have not studied it. And as soon as there is a chemical imbalance in the body, as soon as there is nervous pressure or tension in the body, the peace of mind is lost. A person who has not discovered the art and science of keeping the body in the beauty of health, and in the music of harmony between the muscles, the nerves, the glands and so on, the beauty of keeping the spine erect, the dignity of keeping it erect, keeping the body straight, not stiff, but supple and pliable, how can he have peace of mind ? Unless we discover that, the distortions and twists in the physical organism are bound to get reflected in the mental attitudes. So one has to lay the right foundation on the physical level. Not of acceptance or rejection.

Some people accept and the younger generation goes into a wholesale rejection. Both are unscientific. One has to discover the content in one's life as a scientific approach. Never accept nor reject anything unless you question the validity thereof and test it in your own life. That is what we need. A revolutionary approach. Then comes the mind. We do need a first-hand acquaintance with this sophisticated cerebral organ, which we call the brain, the mind, and we live through it from morning till night. We receive stimulii through the sense-organs. They are carried over as sensations through the brain and the brain-cells interpret those sensations and react to them. Those reactions are called thoughts or feelings or sentiments and these reactions have been fed into the human brain systematicially.

The Hindus have had one way of feeding thoughts and feelings, sentiments, reflexes—voluntary, involuntary conditioned reflexes through the ways of physical and psychological behaviour. The Hindus have faith in one pattern, the Muslims in another, the Catholics in still another, the Buddhists in still another. There have been systematic ways of feeding in. So what we call the thoughts and the feelings, the sentiments and emotions, the opinions, values, the theories, please do see that they do not belong to the individuals. They are the products of collective human activity. If they have not been standardised and organised, if they have not been regimented, the Hindus collectively would not react to a situation in one way and the Muslims would not react collectively in another way. The Catholics would not react in one way and the Communists in another way. Communism, socialism—they have been conditioning the human brain for the last hundred years or so, 150 years perhaps, in one way.

Thus thinking and feeling and willing, all these are mechanistic activities. They are reactions to the sensations, to the impressions. As long as we live through the mind, we are in the realm of activity, we are passively reacting and we do not know what action is, action, which is the flower blossoming into the soil of wholeness, the totality of your being. It is not partial. It is not fragmentary. It is not an intellectual or psychological movement. It is the spontaneous expression of the totality of that individual. That is action, Action is qualitatively different from activity. Activity is the reaction of the mind or the brain to the sensations created by impressions received by the sense organ. So there is nothing to feel proud of our thoughts and feelings, the values, the theories, the opinions. As long as the mind moves it is mechanical movement.

I cannot cover the whole subject in one evening, but I would like to go around it very slowly so that we do have a look at the

whole canvass of human life. The mind and the brain moves
mechanically. Knowledge and experience get reduced to certain
chemicals which are contained in the brain cells. I wonder if you
have read that knowledge can be extracted from certain brain-
cells and be injected into another human brain. Extraction of
knowledge and memory and injection of that same knowledge and
memory has become possible. You must have read about the
computers and the electronic brains. They also have power to
receive, to retain and to invoke. The electronic brains, they do
miraculous things. To watch them do things, to watch them
draw paintings, to watch them compose poems, to watch them
examine the examination papers of university students, not only
the papers of mathematics but papers of languages !! To watch
them play chess !! They even are capable of doing permutations
and combinations of certain patterns of behaviour fed into them
and so on. So all these functions of reception, retention and invo-
cation which man was feeling very proud of in the last couple of
centuries have been proved beyond doubt to be mechanical things,
they are mechanistic movements.

The second limitation of the movement of mind or brain is,
it has to work through certain concepts and symbols. You know-
when you receive a telegraphic message—it is a code language and
then in the office it is decoded. The electronic brains, the computers also receive message in code language. You have to decipher,
decode it. In the same way, the concepts and symbols are the
code-languages of the brain. They are the code-languages of the
word 'psyche'. You use the arithmetical figures, numbers like
1, 2, 3 upto 10 and the whole mathematics is based on the relationship of these numbers. Have these numbers real existence ? Or,
they are the inventions of human genius to construct certain
sciences.

You know that the whole science of geometry, the whole
development of engineering is based on the supposition of a point,
which has no magnitude, which has no length. The whole science
of music is based on the seven basic notes. The word we are now
using is also a symbol. So the mind or the brain cannot function
without the help of concepts and symbols. And you will be surprised

to find that what we call the 'me', the 'self', the 'ego', the 'I'-consciousness, is also a concept. What we call time is a concept.
We use time for the convenience of collective relationship. You
say 8 0' clock, 9 0' clock, two hours, twentyfour hours, days, weeks,
months and years. But are there any years, and weeks and months
in reality ?

Life exists in pure isness. There are no divisions in life.
Man has created these divisions for the convenience of his relationship and then he has forgotten that time was a concept, that
these minutes, hours and days are the symbols of those concepts.
He forgets that the to-days and to-morrows have no existence in
reality. They are the creations of his imagination. Of course,
these concepts and symbols have enriched, they have given a colour
to human relationship. There is a beauty about them. If we know
that they are symbols and they are not reality, we would be free.
When a symbol or a concept is confused with reality that very
symbol becomes a bondage.

There is nothing like bondage in life, but confusing the very
concepts that man created for the convenience of relationship with
reality, with life brings about bondage. Man has created the concepts of to-morrow. He has created the illusion of yesterday and
then he gets bound in the memory of yesterday and dreams of tomorrow, both of which have no existence at all. What is, is now
in the present, here. In the nowness, life exists. If there is any
immortality or eternity, it is in the present. So the second limitation of the brain is, it cannot function without time, space and
'I-consciousness', the ego, the self, the me which is a creation,
which is a concept. And forgetting that we are using the concepts, treating them as if they are the content of life, man gets bound
in his own concepts and then he starts weeping 'I am in bondage,
you come and liberate me'.

Bondage is not a fact of life. It is the ignorance, it is again
the mistake of confusing relative things with absolute reality, of
confusing symbols and concepts with the reality of life. That confusion has to be understood. Then he will not become depressed,
frustrated and cry in fear, possessed and obsessed by fear and wait

for someone to come and liberate him, to illumine him. Illumination or liberation is as much a myth as bondage is a myth and we have to understand the nature of these myths. So when one understands that thought and feeling is only the result of collective human activity, of our ways of behaviour—that is to say, this civilization, culture, are only our collective ways of behaviour. There is nothing to feel proud of them. Then it will be possible for us to look at the anger, the jealousy, the envy, when they come up. To look at them. To-day we are not capable of looking at them.

As soon as the anger comes up, I am angry. I identify myself, the feeling of 'I am', the feelihg of the life within me, I identify that with the anger, with the jealousy, the hatred, the annoyance, the feeling of elatedness, the feeling of pleasure, pain. I identify myself with that. So I am not acquainted with what is happening within me. So I do feel the beginning of personal discovery is in the acquaintance with the movement of mind, not studying books of psychology, somewhere in isolation, theories about the ego, the self, the soul, the theories of Freud and Yung or whosoever he be, the oriental or the occidental, but we have to get acquainted with our own mind.

One should spend sometime everyday in one's own company and watch the movement of the mind, see how the movement of mind makes one a slave, see the slavery to the mind, to the mechanical movement of the mind.

Instead of hunting for peace, instead of hunting for silence, one has to find out why one is restless. Where is the source of lack of peace, lack of harmony, lack of love ? We have to find that out too. It is the ignorance of the known that leads to the bondage. So one has to get acquainted first hand. Then we will be able to look at the anger. When we look at it, when it gets exposed to the light of my awareness, to the light of my consciousness, it loses the grip over me. Uptil now I have been identifying myself with it. Now I am looking at it. There is a space between the anger, the jealousy or whatever it is, and one who is watching.

Thus the momentum of the sub-conscious, the momentum of the past, the momentum of the known loses its grip over me. It is there. It does not get eliminated in one hour or in one night.

It is there. It has the momentum of thousands of years behind it. But it loses the grip. It loses the sting as it were and then one gets into a sense of freedom from that slavery, that momentum of the sub-conscious, unconscious, the slavery of the mind. The moment you can look at your bondage, you are already in the event of freedom. To be aware of the bondage is the beginning of freedom.

Understanding the content of bondage is the beginning of freedom. Freedom is not something separate to be attained, to be achieved. Freedom or liberation is not something to be cultivated. It is not different. It is not different from the bondage. One has to look at it, understand it and that very understanding explodes into freedom. They are not two different events, and we have to look at these not in isolation, not sitting somewhere in the corner of a room, but from morning till night to be in the state of watchfulness, in the state of observation, without condemning what is coming up or without accepting what is coming up. Just observing it, seeing the speed, the momentum, the electronic speed with which thoughts come, watching the intervals between the two thoughts.

If one can be sensitive to the intervals between two thoughts, between two feelings, then that very sensitivity to the silence of that interval is going to strengthen the anaemic minds. So the second step is to get acquainted with the mind, with the ego and to be free of that momentum. It is an arduous task because we do not like to be attentive all the time. We want to go on repeating certain habits and to be watchful, to be mindful needs energy, needs attention. You cannot do a thing out of habit. Then right from the moment you open your eyes, up to the moment you go to bed and close your eyes, you have to be watchful, to be vigilant.

Vigilance is the price that one has to pay and we like to be slow, to be lethargic, to be sluggish, to follow certain habits, to follow certain patterns, repeat them. Repetition is second-hand living. To follow a habit is not to live first hand at all, and all the time spent is not to live first-hand at all, and all the time spent in following patterns of habits is really lost. We have not lived then. To live is to move with the movement of life, to be attentive every moment. So when one has done that, then in the very

7

act of watching and observing the dimension of silence has come to life. Because when you are observing, you are not analysing, you are not interpreting, you are not accepting, you are not reacting according to the dictates of the mind. So in the very act of observation, when observation is sustained as a state of being, it makes a tremendous difference. Then the ego, I-consciousness is not functioning. Silence as a dimension comes to life.

Silence is not something negative. It is not a vacuum. It is not a void. But as soon as the total mind, with ego at the centre and knowledge at the circumference or the periphery, is quiet, the energy which is beyond the ego, which is beyond the brain, becomes operative. Man, I say, has not discovered the totality of his being. He has not found out the roots of his energy. Now when the body is quiet and when the mind is not functioning, when one is in the state of egolessness, then energy at the roots of our being becomes operative. Uptil now it was scattered, it was dissipated. Now it has gone back to its centre, to its source. It is there in its wholeness, in its totality and now it begins to move as the whole.

Energy is the principle of intelligence. It is never static. It is infinite motion. We know the movement of the body, conditioned by space and time, we know the movement of brain which is conditioned by time and thought. Man has measured the movement, the physical movement, through space and time. Man has measured the movement of thought, the vibrations of thought, the colours, the frequency of those vibrations and so on. These are only partial movements. Beyond this is the real movement of life. Man has not yet measured it—the infinite motion of pure energy, which is intelligence, which is sensitivity, which is love. Give it any name you like. And divinity is the fragrance of that totality, of that wholeness.

The value of human life is because of its potential divinity. Each one of us is an expression of that divinity. We are not aware of it. Life is divine. To divide life into material and spiritual, to fragment it is an unscientific attitude. Even if you analyse matter, you arrive at energy—vibrations of energy, that is all. You may go on analysing matter and no logic and no mathematics is going to help you to find out the ratio between the mass of a molecule

$$e = mc^2$$

of matter and quantum of energy contained in it. So life is energy and energy is the divinity. It cannot be imprisoned in any name and form. You may give it a name and form for some purpose of studying the mind. You may give names and forms and use them romantically, poetically, aesthetically. But the totality of life will never be imprisoned in any form which has to be located in space and time. So that totality of energy, which is the infinite intelligence and sensitivity, that is the true nature, is the true source of our being.

It is not possible to go into the elaboration of how perception goes through a qualitative change as soon as one is in the state egolessness. It is a non-dual perception, immediate, direct, without the intervention of an idea, without the intervention of a thought, without the intervention of a name, the direct, immediate perception of reality. It is a non-dual perception, unrelated to time and space. And how the state of egolessness living in that dimension of explosive silence trans-forms the quality of response ! Now we respond through a motive, through a purpose, through an idea, through a theory, through values, through opinions. So our reactions are not spontaneous. They are polluted and they are contaminated. But then the non-dual perception leads to a spontaneous response and spontaneity is the content of love.

It may sound very high-flown but it is the pure and simple statement of fact. I am not a capable person to pour the beauty of life into these rigid words, The medium of verbal communication is one of the most feeble mediums of ʳcommunication. But words are grasped. The word is something material and when one uses the words, one has to communicate through words. One finds it so diffiicult and yet we have to communicate through words ! So a non-dual perception and a spontaneous response through immense sensitivity and infinite intelligence, response through love is a new dimension. Man has to grow into that dimension. The challenge to-day is the challenge to grow into the maturity of egoless state of consciousness not for a few Yogis and Sanyāsīs, not for those who retire to caves and mountains in the Himalayas or monasteries somewhere. It is a life and death question for you and me.

Thought has been used. Mind has been indoctrinated in infinite ways. Indoctrination into different theories and ideologies does not lead us anywhere. We may talk about a classless society, exploitationless society; but man, the savage at the core of our being, full of animal instincts and drives, wanting to own, to possess, to dominate remains the same. He throws all idelogies, all values, all norms to winds. In the democratic countries or the socialist countries, it is individual man, lustful, dominating savage, who is throwing to wind all theories, all cultures, civilization. So the crisis is in the individual psyche and we have to face it. When the dimension of human consciousness beyond brain, beyond mind comes into operation (and the time has come to grow into that dimension) then we will be free of the animal instincts, the I-consciousness, which is the fortress of defence-mechanism, Then we shall live and move out of that new dimension. Then only man will be free to love his fellow human beings, to behave as a mature human being. Now we are behaving like human animals. Then we will become mature human beings. Then we will replace anger, hatred and jealousy by love and co-operation.

To-day if I talk about the dynamic force of love, people just don't believe. If you talk about a revolution, brought about through the dynamism of love and co-operation, they say, no it cannot be. You have to teach people to hate. You have to teach them, provoke their jealousy and hatred against one another. Hatred and anger, jealousy and violence have been used as motivation forces for revolutions and now is the challenge to replace them by the dynamic force of love and co-operation. Then we will bring about socio-economic, political, cultural, international changes in a decent, humane way.

How can man talk of love and friendship in the temple, in the church and the mosque and come out and teach fellow human beings to hate one another in the name of nation, country, ideology, religion ? I fail to understand. And we have to resolve this contradiction. We have to get over this skizofrania from which we are suffering. So, for me, the symptoms of problems may be on the fringes of political, economic and social level, but the malady is deep-rooted in the quality of consciousness. We have to face the challenge there. And I do feel all human beings are capable of doing that, not only the privileged few. The consummation of human growth is the state of freedom and love. And I say this as one of you, living and moving amongst you, carrying out the daily responsibility of any ordinary human being.

I am very grateful to those who have organised such a beautiful meeting and given me an opportunity of meeting you and I am very grateful to each one of you who have listened to me with such rapt attention. I am also grateful to Mataji who gracefully came this morning not to receive me, but I think she has blessed me in the morning as soon as I landed here at Trincomalee airport and it has been very kind of her to come to this meeting also. Let me hope that all of us feel the seriousness of the situation the world over that man is passing through. Let us seriously take up the challenge of discovering how to live as a human being. May we be blessed with the urge of that personal discovery of Truth. May we be blessed with the sustained seriousness, which is vitally necessary to conduct the personal enquiry.

Thank you all.

(8th March, 1971)

I wonder what kind of talk you will expect of me this morning. This is an officers' meeting. It has been many years since I have not been addressing Government officers in any country. I did it in Colombo nearly after twelve years and this happens to be the second meeting. I wonder whether you would like to listen to something fundamental, not specially critical of any personnel, or any system, but fundamental about the problems in human relationship and what we as individuals can do, not to aggravate the evil side but to contribute individually to good to peace, to law and order and so on.

You might be observing as I do that the issue of maintaining law and order in society is becoming more and more complicated, in democratic countries, in the dictatorial countries, cov atries which call themselves socialist countires, theocratic countries, secular countries, everywhere it is the same. Let us go back to the theory of Social Contract by Rousseau that you have studied regarding the question as to how human society came into existence. Animals live in herds, birds fly and flock together in groups, but human beings came together to create a society. Has it ever struck us to discriminate between groups, herds and society ?

How does the human society come into existence ? I won't go into the whole theory of social contract where individuals willingly accepted to put restrictions on their liberty for the sake of security and also management of mutual relationship. It is very interesting to find out how society evolved. It has not come into existence in a day. Man has struggled to come to the present state. A society is a group of individuals who are conscious, who are aware that they are living together and in exchange for the security that this togetherness gives to them or confers upon them, they have to sacrifice some part of their liberty. Where do the restrictions on liberty come and they are justified and where do the restrictions become intrusions on privacy and liberty ? That has to be studied very deeply and it is one of the most interesting subjects to be studied by the lovers of freedom and lovers of life—lovers who respect and revere life.

I have mentioned this in the very beginning because administration is concerned not with ruling over human beings but managing human relationship. There is a difference between the two. Administration of human beings that used to be the way with the administrator, the rulers, the kings, the princes, the emperors, in the East, in the West, right from China upto Europe and even in America before Americans became free, is not our concern here. Just as you use whips against animals, rules and regulations were used in place of those whips for the sake of administration. The interest of the ruler had the priority over the interest of those who were ruled. But the relationship between the ruler and the ruled, the administrator and the administrated went through a radical change with the concepts and theories of democracy and socialism. The relationship was no more of ruling over the people, but management of things that are necessary for the human being. There has been a change from administration to managment in the concept of real democracy where there should be a Government of the people, for the people and by the people, where people are to be ruled by their consent, not implicit but explicit consent.

The change in the dynamics and the change in the dimension, in the relationship between the two has to be taken notice of. Unfortunately, as I observed in India (I could not talk about your country because this is my first visit to your country and I am not sufficiently acquainted with the trends here), though India became free, yet the change in relationship has not come. Nobody helped the bureaucracy, nobody helped the officers to realise that they were not rulers of the Indian people any more. They were administrators and yet not rulers. You know the mentality of the ruler, a superiority complex, a kind of idea of being the master. That was with the British people. They behaved in India as the master does. But there is no master as far as the Indian people at large are concerned. Nobody helped the officers to realise this.

I do not know if anybody has helped the people in Ceylon to realise the difference in the dimension that comes over the political independence. The relationship must go through a change so that the gap petween the ruler and the ruled, the administrator and the administrated has got to become less and less. It has to be replaced by co-operation, by mutual respect so that the rulers become the real servants of the people. That is the crust of the whole issue in democracy. And the people who are illiterate, who are starving, they are also not educated nor are the officers educated. They do not get the orientation nor do the people get orientation that with the right to vote which they have to exercise, they are really becoming the sovereigns of the country.

The sovereignty of the people, expressed in their consent, is the foundation of democracy. But there are no people. Where are the people ? There are masses of human beings ignorant about the whole meaning of democracy, ignorant about the meaning of socialism. They do not know. They are starving. There is even the concept of caste, untouchables, superiority, the class superiority, the caste superiority, superiority through education, degrees, qualifications, superiority through money and the power that money brings, superiority of the political power which really the people invest in the officers, in the ministers, in the members of parliament. But the sovereign people are the most ignorant—in Pakistan, in India, may be perhaps even in your country, in the Middle East.

I have travelled much excepting Saudi Arabia and U. A. R.—(United Arab Republic) Where are the people ? People have not been created. We need a people, not the mass of individuals who can be frightened, who can be terrorised, intimidated, who can be tempted and bribed with money and made to serve as voters. Votes can be snatched away from poor people, for 2 rupees, 3 rupees, 5 rupees. I have been a witness unto many elections in India.

It is the mockery of democracy unless we create a people and that people can be created through adult education and literacy campaign. They did it in China after 1919. The University students, the professors, the teachers, whosoever were educated did it. But the countries in South East Asia, including India, did not do it. I hope that these little countries, these tiny countries, will not commit the mistakes which their neighbours have committed.

It is vitally necessary to create the people out of the mass of human beings, out of the mass of inertia. Passivity has to be mobilised. So I have been talking about this in Colombo in the student's meeting and also the public meetings. Let us not talk of democracy. It is a paper democracy. It has no life unless you create the people by educating them to the importance, the sanctity of the right to vote. The right to vote is something sacred. It is the chastity of the women. It must not be violated, under any name whatsoever and then again a new orientation is to be given to the officers so that the dimension of relationship is changed, so that they will be dealing with the human being in their respective departments with greater respect, greater affection. They will not allow the people to get contaminated through bribery, out of fear, out of temptation. Hence the responsibility of the educated people, those who are in the offices, those who are in the Universities, those who become members of Senate, Parliament. That responsibility, for a generation or two, is going to be very great. Unless they pay the price of vigilance, democracies and republics and socialist countries, will just be decorations on paper. They will be like dead corpses decorated or decoration of something dead. It is not vulgar, but it is something drastic, terrible.

Small countries like Ceylon, Indonesia, Korea, Vietnam and also small countries in the Middle East, you will be surprised to realise, they hold a very important place now in the power balance in the whole world. It is not the monstrously huge countires like Russia and United States of America who hold the power balance. It is the small countries, significantly enough. I am not going to go into world history. Since 1945 how the scales of power have been changed, how the power is coming more and more into the hands of the coloured people from the white race; and from the big countries and big blocs of countries to small countries ! The Colombo pact after the Chinese aggression in India (as they call it aggression, I belong to no country though I was born in India; I feel, I belong to the whole of humanity), had its impact on India, Pakistan and China as you might have noticed. Thus the small countries will have to be extremely careful in the way they evolve and in the way they work out their economic and political frameworks.

I would now refer to a couple of challenges that are facing us in Asia and Africa. There will be diverse problems. I feel that there will crystallise a new class, a class of bureaucracy, a class of officers, as it did in Yogoslavia. You know the brave Yogoslavians and their whole fight against Austria, their brave stand against Russia and their efforts at breaking a new path in implementing the philosophy of Marx and Lenin and Angles. I spent about a couple of months there, studying there what they have done in 1959. They could not avoid a few points. The first was, eliminating the economic exploitation and eliminating the capitalist class. But the bureaucratic class had come, composed of those who have to wield power in the name of 'State'.

It is easy to nationalise means and instruments of production, nationalise the geographical resources. Nationalisation has been the slogan very intimately related to the theory of socialism. I won't go into the propriety of it. But that was accepted by the Yugoslavians, i. e. State ownership of the means and instruments of production. But those who had to wield the power in the name of the state, they were after all individuals. They were human beings. They had not gone through a qualitative change in their attitudes towards money, towards ownership, towards property. So the relationship to money and property was the same. The communes were created. But the desire to acquire, to own and to possess in the name of communes, was the same. The profit motive was looked upon as the only incentive to productive labour by the young people in Yugoslavia. Boys and girls would not take to any specialisation. "When we are going to get the same remuneration as the unskilled labour why should we study ?"—this was their attitude.

Remuneration to each according to his capacity and to each according to the needs, that was the talk before the revolution. But after the revolution when the country became free, the people had to deal with the resources, had to deal with the means and instruments of production, they had to deal with the money, the work, that the country was producing per capita, per acre, per unit of production. So nobody had tried to change the quality of consciousness, to change the attitudes towards property, towards ownership. Nobody had studied the cultural problems of incentive in a socialist country.

They have changed over from capitalism and feudalism to socialism. They have changed socio-economic structure, political structure. What do we do with the psychological structure inhabiting the psyche of each individual ? So the ratio of remuneration between the unskilled and the skilled labour in Yugoslavia from 1948 to 1953 was 1 : 5, and between 1953 and 1959 it went up to 1 : 13 because nobody would take up engineering, medicine, nobody would specialise. The young generation was reacting in apathy, indifference. So the Government had to widen the gap. I am trying to bring out a very important point and that is, why do you change over from capitalism to socialism ?

It is vitally necessary to change the outer structure—socio-economic, political, cultural. They have got to be changed. There cannot be two opinions about it. But what do we do with the individuals ? How do we educate and reorient the whole psychological approach ? If we do not do that then changing the outer expression, changing the collective patterns does not take you very far.

We have studied the history of the last fifty years of Soviet Russia. You might have studied the tension between Russia and China, the competition for leadership in the two huge countries. You see the leadership of the communist countries in the world and the leadership also of the non-communist countries, the competition between the two, the tensions on borders. The sensitive, explosive border between Russia and China is the most eloquent expression that unless human beings simultaneously change the quality of their individual psyche and consciousness, changing the collective patterns of behaviour, and changing the socio-economic and political structure does not take you very far.

Thus the challenge for you and me in the developing countries in Asia is of finding out a way of total revolution. Changing the outer but simultaneously changing the inner too. We the educated have to realise that the roots of all aggression, exploitation, injustice, violence are in our heart. The roots are in the individual psyche. It is easy to condemn the war in Vietnam, the violence in East Pakistan, the violence in India, the battle in the Middle East, the quarrel between Jordan and Isreal, Egypt and Isreal.

It is very easy to condemn the corruption in various countries. Do I look at the corruption in my own heart ? When somebody comes to bribe me and flatter me how do I feel ? If I want to get my interest fulfilled at any cost, I do not worry about democracy then. I do not worry about socialism when I have to get a job for my nephew, for my niece, for my brother, for my uncle. I go and fiatter any M. P. or go to any minister, I get it done. If I have to build a house, if I want to have a telephone and I am not getting it quickly, whatever I do becomes justified in the name of my self-interest and I say that the world is like that, what csn I do ? Each one says that.

Each one out of millions says that the world is like that. Everybody says when someone else is doing, why not I ? That is how we come to it. My getting angry in the office with the superior, with the inferior, with the boss, with the clerks, with the peons, whoever he be, the jealousy that I use in my work; the anger that I express in my daily behaviour in the five hours in the office, 8 hours in the office, the violence that I use against my wife, my children, my husband—is it not ghastly ? Is it less criminal than the war waged in the battle fields of Vietnam, Laos and Cambodia ? It is a question of degree only.

Hence one has to shoulder the responsibility of rooting out the seed of violence and exploitation from one's own heart. We may like it or we may not like it. But you and I, perhaps even the next generation, will have to live a very austere life if we want to eliminate poverty and starvation from our country. We cannot indulge in the dreams of well-to-do rich life for ourselves and talk in the same breath about elimination of poverty and starvation and injustice from society. After a generation or two, perhaps the country would have increased the national wealth to such an extent that this austerity may not be necessary. But like our forefathers for political independence, we will have to struggle in austerity and simplicity.

One who dreams of personal wealth, property and richness cannot become an eliminator of poverty and starvation from society. We are all potential capitalists in our heart. When we do not succeed and the dreams are not fulfilled, the unsuccessful rich are the poor and the succcessful poor become the rich. That is the only difference. So I do feel that it is necessary for us to look at this issue of austerity and simplicity. I am not saying that all should become nuns and monks or Sanyāsīs, not at all. That is again another extreme. But to live where we are, to live in truth and justice, as far as far as we can, as far as we human beings can, not converting the weaknesses and the crimes of others as a defence for our behaviour. The moment we will give up using the behaviour of other people as a defence for our weaknesses, the moment we give up that, then the democracy will come to life from the paper democracy. It has become a living one.

That is the challenge for the whole Middle East and the South East Asia. Nobody likes to accept the sense of responsibility. Everybody likes to relegate the responsibility to others and here I come in the name of people. For me God exists in the form of human beings and He is to be worshipped there. The reverence for life has got to be expressed there aad at the table where I work in the office, in the bus when I travel, at home with my wife and husband and children. It is to be expressed there, not only in the churches, in temples and the mosques. So we need a humility to shoulder the responsibility of this austere task. Perhaps a generation or two will have to do that.

The second thing that I would like to emphasise is the second challenge as I see it. The countries in Asia and Africa have to discover an altogether different pattern of industrial revolution from the one that we have seen in Europe and America. I have lived with the most affluent people—the people in Sweden, the people in Switzerland, the people in America and have seen their nauseating affluence. The cultural problems of affluence-stricken countries are not less serious than those of the poverty-stravation-stricken countries, and that affluence they have created at the cost of their inner peace and joy. I am not going to talk against affluence. It is absolutely necessary to satisfy decently, aesthetically all the basic needs of life and here we are living in Asia not even at subsistance level. We are living at a sub-human level. Then we have to go a long way. But how would we go ?

When you go ahead, how do you take the first step ? The first step determines the nature of the arrival. The means determines and decides the nature of the end. The end is not collectively different from the means. Now, in the industrial revolution that took place in Europe a couple of centuries ago and perhaps 120 years ago in United States of America, they were emphasising mass production, centralised production, large units of production. The land-man-ratio was responsible for it. They did not have the surplus human labour which is available to the people of Asia and Africa, that human labour which we are cursing, we could convert into a blessing, if mobilised properly.

Thus the word 'industrial revolution' in Europe and America was capital-oriented, based on money and capital, not on mobilisation of man-power because they did not have it. Mobilisation of man-power, mobilisation of the initiative of the individuals has absolutely been unknown in the West, even in the socialist countries in Europe. They have copied the capital-intensive economic planning from the hangover of the capitalist system still existing in the socialist countries.

Hence I do feel that we will need a labour-intensive economic planning. We will need an industrial revolution not based on centralised production, centralisation of economic power, huge units of production and so on. It was relevant in the 18th and 19th century when people could capture colonies and make economic empires. They could exploit the colonies. Now the days of colonies and empires are over. We are not going to capture markets overseas. That was the problem in Yugoslavia in 1959. What to do with the surplus in Corsia and Serbia ? They have lots of surplus. The Montanigo and other constituencies and other states in southern Yugoslavia had no money to purchase what Serbia and Corsia of north was producing and they did not know where to dump the goods. So they had to find out how to export. Though the Yugoslavians needed it in the south, they could not sell it in the south and they had to find out markets overseas in Italy and France and other countries because otherwise they would not get the price.

What I am trying to say, Sir, just indicate very briefly, in a very short talk is that we will have to find out a different way of

industrial revolution. Perhaps we will have to decentralise indust-
ries, not centralise them. We will have to mobilise the individual
initiative, employ the human labour and use machinery to supple-
ment it, to complement it and not to replace it. This is not speaking against science and technology. We will have to use science
and technology. We cannot commit the mistake that the Indians
committed. Gandhi had pointed out the way. They did not listen.

The dazzling of the so-called material progress and affluence
of the West had blinded the vision of the Indian people and they
started begging from all over the world and basing all their five-year
plans on foreign aid with the invisible string. Visibly the strings
were denied. Invisibly they were allright there. You can mortgage
the whole country in the name of foreign aid. You will never be
able to repay it. I do not know how they are going to repay, if at
all they do want to repay. So you ignore the sense of self-respect of
the people, you go on feeding the people on what you beg of other
countries. The sense of self-respect of the people whithers away in
no time. Already the passivity and intertia due to slavery of centu-
rise is there and then they base all the plans on foreign aid, on
capital-intensive industrial revolution.

We must have industrial revolution. All right have it. But
why must you have it the way Europeans have had it, or the way
Americans have had it ? Why not find out your own way of appl-
ying science and technology, even your nuclear energy ? Why not
have small units of production ? Why must you uproot villagers
and provoke them to the curse of urbanisation ? Urbanisation is not
the only indication of civilization and culture. So why not provide
small units of production in the rural area on a zonal or regional
basis, complementing and supplementing the human and the animal
labour ? So we will need much less investment per capita to give
jobs to the poor people. We will not feed them on what we beg
and borrow. We will not create in them a mentality of depending
upon the world. The psychology of dependence, is it not a kind of
slavery ?

This is a small country. You have not got the staggering dimension that the Indians have to their economic problems. Perhaps in

this country, the educated people could talk to their rulers, talk to their leaders and say that they need a new planning, they need a different kind of industrial revolution. Let us not beg. Let us not borrow. Let us not feed the people, but mobilise their initiative. Unless this initiative of the individual citizen is mobilized, democracy has no meaning. They will cry out for Welfare State or, they will cry out for socialisation of everything and wanting everything in return from the government.

The name 'public sector' appears enchanting till we put everything under the public sector and see what it does. The production in the public sector is always poorer than the private sector. Why ? The result of the co-operative movement is disappointing—Why ? Because the quality of consciousness, the psychological approaches to priorities in the lives of individuals have not changed.

Thus this immense task of creating an independent approach to economic problems is absolutely necessary, not copying from the East or the West. So this is a challenge to the creative genius of the people, the younger people in Asia, and I am very carefully and attentively watching since my arrival, the trends in your country whatever little I can do by studying the newspapers, discussing with people. How this country is going to shape its future, how they are drafting the new constitution and how are they going to implement it ? Drafting is easier, implementing is going to be a tough task and implementation with the consent of the people, that is the test of culture and civilization.

Thus this is the second problem, the second challenge to the creative genius of finding out an entirely new approach to industrialisation. We do need industrialisation. But it will be an agro-centred industrialisation. I have worked in the villages of India, collected about 200,000 acres of land in the Land Gift Movement and distributed them. While terracing the hills for cultivation, building dams to the rivers, I have tried labour-intensive planning in Assam, in Orissa, in Tamilnadu and so on.

There is tremendous potentiality in the innate intelligence of the villager if we give him a chance. I have told your brothers in Colombo that once I was in North Assam; and the officers, the engineers told me that they could not dam a certain river, that a

dam could not be built there. The river was Suvarnasree, north
of Brahmaputra, in the district North Lakhimpur. I collected the
villagers, the heads of the Panchayats from twenty-five villages
and talked to them. I said I cannot accept the word 'impossible'.
Shall we walk round and see ? Are you willing to walk with me
through the forest, by the bank of the river ? We will do it for weeks
together. There must be some span which will heed to our efforts
of building a dam and those twenty-five heads of the Panchayats
accepted. And we, about thirty-five of us, marched through the
forest for three weeks. I was wandering through the forest, by
the banks of the river; a way out of the problem may not be written
in the books, but if the river has done so much damage to all the
villages around, we must find out one. How can a living human
being accept defeat so easily, because the books do not tell it ? In
the end, the villagers found it out. I had more faith in them. They
found it out.

We invited villagers from 25 to 30 villages; 300 to 500 persons
were working with me in that bed of the river. We could finish
it in about two and a half months and then I invited the Chief
Minister of the State to come and visit it. He said how could you
do it ? I said come and see. The villagers have done it. The
innate intelligence, the faith in the people, respect for their reason,
faith in their goodness, it works miracles, I tell you. Not that it
is a path of roses. There are thorns too. They will prick and the
feet will bleed and so will the heart. But that is a part of the
whole game. So building up the nation is not building dams and
huge units of production, but the building of the character of the
people, their respect for freedom, their self respect, their self-reliance, that is the essence of freedom, that is the essence of socialism,
that is the essence of democracy, whatever name you may use,
'That is the second point I have indicated. I had not thought that
I would take so much time. But instead of diluting what I have
to say, I thought it better to concentrate upon fundamental issues.
I would come to the last point and conclude my communication
with you.

The last point is of human relationship. Leaving aside the
socio-economic structure, political set-ups, our mutual relation-
8

ships—how are they to-day all the world over ? Why does man get irritated so quickly ? Why does he lose the balance of his mind and the beauty and grace of his behaviour ? We have till now dealt, in fundamentals, in essence, with the outer structure, which is outside the skin. I am coming to the inner structure now. I am coming to the issue of mind.

You and I use the mind from morning till night. We work through it and we can use the knowledge that we have acquired in the universities efficiently. We may have degrees, qualifications. We may be very efficient and competent officers, competent ministers. What happens to the quality of our relationships with others ? The way we look at them, the way we react to their behaviour,—why that quality is so poor ? After all if a person gets angry half a dozen times in eight hours, gets irritated half a dozen times in those 8 oours, behaves indifferently, gets shaken by jealouy and envy, half a dozen times, what is happening to him ?

Have you observed that when you get angry, anger works havoc upon the whole being ? Have you ever observed how it contracts your intestines, the whole digestive process, how it gene- rates extra heat which rushes to your head ? Just a moment, one moment of anger and look what it is doing. Extra heat that is rushing towards the brain, the tenseness in the optical nerves, the tension in the auditory nerves, and you lose the whole balance. The metabolical disturbance aod the chemical disturbance in the body upsets the whole balance and one behaves in a way which is not very behoving to a cultured person. In that moment of anger, the glance that escapes you, the gestures that escape you, the words that escape would make any one of you feel ashamed of it later on. This is momentary insanity. It is a kind of neurotic tendency. We may question, then we may say "Oh ! it is human nature, getting angry, geting annoyed, getting irritated, this living through from morning till night". This is not the way to live Does it not mean that we do not know how to use the mind ?

If a person is driving a car and he cannot use gears properly, the brakes he cannot use properly, he does not know how much pressure to give on the escalator, he does not know how to use the mobil-oil and the petrol and so on. It does create friction. The choke-pipe is not working properly. You say the person does not know how to handle the car. It is a beautiful make and yet he does not know how to drive the car. You do not allow him to drive the car. But we drive our minds and brains without even studying and getting acquainted with their mechanism.

Half the misery is due to the ignorance of the mechanism of the mind, the chemistry of thoughts and emotions. And these temporary so-called transitory imbalances, when they visit and shatter your nervous system through the eight hours, then everything goes out. when you go home, the tensions work, they seek their own relief and the people cannot understand why you are so short-tempered, why you are so irritated. But we do not find any immediate cause to associate with your behaviour, and you yourself feel surprised. So I do feel that it is necessary to study what the mind is, how it works. When you think a thought what is happening ? It is a movement within. When you feel an emotion, it is a movement of what is taking place within.

As one studies physics and chemistry and biology, why not study the mechanism of mind and thought ? Then one will discover that thoughts and emotions do not belong to any individuals. They are not your thoughts and your emotions, your feelings and your reflections. They are all products of collective human activity. They have been produced carefully, sophisticated carefully through centuries, by man. The Hindu way of reacting, even among the Hindus, the Tamilian way of reacting, the Shaivaites,' the Vaishnavites,' the Buddhists' way of reacting, the communist way of reacting, the Catholic way, the Muslim way and so on have all been. They are all ways of behaviour. We mistake them for thoughts. They do not belong to us and that is why we take so much pride.

All the pride and vanity in thoughts and emotions and opinions and theories will drop away like the winter leaves the moment we know that they are mechanical movements. Cerebral movement is a mechanical movement. It is very interesting to study. Whichever way mind moves, it is a mechanical movement. Using certain symbols, it plays around with the symbol and constructs. As long as mind has to construct with notes, with colours, with numbers, it is a constructive activity. It is not a creative action. So when one studies the mechanism of mind and understands that cerebral movement is nothing marvellous, it is only a mechanical, automatic movement, then this attachment to one's likes and dislikes, one's preferences and prejudices, all this whithers away.

The movement is there. The thoughts, the emotions, the memory is there. It is inside the skin. You cannot linch it away. It will be there. But the attachment, the pride, the vanity, will whither away, It will fade away and then this attitude of feeling superior over others due to certain thoughts and due to certain ways of behayiour—this superiority and inferiority complex, they also will whither away. Then only one can handle the mind, one can handle the reactions of the mind in a scientific way.

Hence I do feel personally that those who work in offices, work in schools, colleges, universities, those who become members of parliament, those who become members of cabinet, it is absolutely and urgently necessary that they study how the mind works. They will have to study how to use the speech, how to use words. Exaggeration is a sophisticated lie, and so many sins are committed by verbal exaggerations. The overstatements, the understatements, unnecessary verbalisation that is gossiping, out of which so many scandals and black-mailing are born,—all this is a misuse of speech, it is an unscientific use of the beautiful capacity to speak. To indulge in gossiping, scandalising, blackmailing, or unnecessary verbalisation, is frittering away the vital energy and then at the end of the day, why am I so tired ? It is not the work that tires, it is the misuse of speech and misuse of minds.

If there is nothing else to do, we sit at home or in the office, we are blankly looking ahead, vaguely playing with the memory of what happened yesterday, day before yesterday, last month, last year. We are violating the modesty of memory by playing around the past experiences. Rumination of the past also means wasting energy. Dreaming about the future is an indulgence in lethargy and sluggishness. So all this unscientific use of mind and speech is the fertile soil in which so many sorrows breed.

This is the responsibility of persons like you and me, who work in the social field, work in government offices, work in universities; it is a great responsibility. To use speech in an austere way, not only the money, but also the mind. Then only, we will not be worn out and tired but we will have the strength to be fresh. We will not be bored but will be ever fresh, Knowing how to use the mind and whenever the use of mind is not necessary to let it alone and live in the silence of mind, which is a dimension of life, this is what we need. Whenever it is necessary to use the mind, we use it out of that silence, that freshness.

I would like to thank the organisers of this meeting who gave this opportunity to me and I would like to thank each one of you who has listened to such an uninteresting, serious talk with such great attention.

Thank you all.

: 10 :

(11th March, 1971)

Question :—How to bring up a child to face the challenges of to-day ?

Answer :—A very interesting question indeed. But the thing is—who is going to bring up the child ? Even if some points are suggested for the consideration of the issue, who is going to bring up the child ? Is the person, or, are the persons capable of meeting the challenges in their own lives ? Unless they are capable of meeting the challenges themselves, do you think they are going to help the child to do so ? So the important question is not somebody suggesting the points for bringing up the children. The important issue is do we love our children ? Are we aware that parenthood is a sacred trust and responsibility ? Parenthood not accepted as a tradition, not as a religious duty, not as a gratification for certain drives and instincts built in the biological organism. So even if I say certain things, may be, it will be looked upon as a 'Utopia'; or, as a symptom of presumptuousness on my part.

When does the bringing up of the child begin ? It begins at the moment of conception. The quality of the consciousness of the child is affected to a very great extent by the way, the attitude, the psychological condition in which the man and the woman meet. If they meet only in lust, it affects the quality of consciousness in one way. If one of the partners is in the mood to dominate, to assert himself or herself, the meeting in domination and the desire to assert affects again the child's consciousness. Who is going to take care of all this ? Do you think the education of the children begins with the K.G. classes ? Does it begin after the child is born ? If it is so, we are labouring under a very expensive illusion.

And when I wander about I see that I am moving specially among the young people who would like to evolve a sex-centred civilization, not only sex-oriented. Something very beautiful is being missed. The man and woman are using each other as an escape from the boredom of life, as an escape from the frustrations and depressions of life, and not in love, not in friendship, not in mutual respect—and that's what generally happens. So the sanctity of parenthood is the foundation on which the right kind of education can begin.

Secondly, the time of bearing the child is important. Now-a-days in the occident women do not like pregnancy. They feel ashamed. They feel tired. It has become a strain. They would like to curtail the period and it has been found possible, it has been made possible to remove the child from the womb in the fourteenth week and bring it up on synthetic blood plasma in a synthetic womb. The whole behaviour of the mother in those nine months, the stresses and strains that she goes through, if she is humiliated, if she is tortured, that also is going to colour the tendencies and the drives in the child. But society has no time to pay attention to all these points. The amount of budget dedicated to defence, the preparation for war, is much more than what is spent on psychological education of the people, on education of the people at large and also on educational institutions.

The whole approach to education has to undergo revolutionary orientation. Otherwise it is no use giving a hint or two here and there. It is not a patch-work to be done The moment the child is born, the comments begin by the parents, by the relatives, by the neighbours; comparing the child, evaluating the child. And parents and the elders think that whatever they say in the presence of the child does not matter. They feel that their attitudes, their glances, their talks, their verbalisations in the presence of the child are not going to affect the child at all. Unfortunately, it is not so. They have their chemical impact upon the child. The child does not know it, and the parents forget it. By the time the child becomes seven or eight, they do not understand why the child hates the father or the mother. The violence, the irritability, the short-temperedness of the child become a problem. But the child has undergone many tortures before he was seven. He has heard so many remarks, comparisons, has been condemned, denied, suppressed, flattered.

All this thoughtless behaviour on the part of the parents in comparing and evaluating unwarrantedly or exhibiting something acquired by them to be exhibited, is wrong. So how to bring up a child is really a fundamental issue needing not only five or ten minute's answer, not needing only one talk, but it is something that we have to go through very deeply and we can't do it in one meeting when there are three or four questions to be answered.

Now, what are the challenges facing us to-day ? I have just pointed out, hinted the content, the implications of the responsibility to bring up a child and when does the question of bringing up arise, where does it begin.

Now let me turn to the other aspect of the question—'to face the challenges of to day". Are we aware of the challenges of the day ? Are we aware that human beings as individuals are nowhere free, in no country, no religion, under no political system ? The problem to-day, the challenge to-day, is of freedom and love in human relationship. Whether it is in a family, or, in a community, a country or international relationship, the basic issue is of basing the human relationships, founding them in freedom and love. So the parents, the teachers will have to find out if they live in psychological freedom, or, they are victims of the authority of traditions, ways of behaviour, ideologies, norms, standards, criteria. Gone are the days when the children would accept everything that their parents say only because they are the parents. Gone are the days when the children would accept everything or anything said by the teacher only because he or she were a teacher. Those days are gone. Nobody is going to bring them back.

Now the children will observe how the parents are living and how the teachers are living and moving at home, in society and if there is anything inconsistent, if there are any contradictions in the lives of the parents and the teachers, we can't expect the children to accept our verdicts, our judgements and fulfil our expectations. The children are bound to refuse. This is the age of revolt and refusal. So, they are bound to refuse to become carbon copies of their parents, fulfil the expectations of the leaders. So, I think it is very necessary for the parents who would like to discuss this issue, to realise that, it is not easy to play with fire. It is taking the life-fire in your hands. To bring up a child, if it is to be done in a conscientious way, if it is to be done in love and respect for the child, then the first thing the parents will have to learn is, that the child is a potential total human being and not a fraction of a human being. Like the small sprouting from the seed of a 'banyan' tree, the child looks so tiny, but he is a whole human being within. It has potentiality of a total human being that is going to blossom and flower in front of your eyes.

So, we will have to respect the tiny children. It is an absolutely new relationship of affection and respect for the child, not pushing them away when we are angry, annoyed, irritated and trying to pat them as you pat your dogs and cats, when you are in a mood to do so. That won't do. So, are we going to have the relationship of respect and affection for the children and help them in growing instead of imposing our ways of behaviour on them ? Education is no more imposition of ways of behaviour. Education will be helping the children to grow. Are we going to give them that freedom ? And to bring them up in freedom is not to expect anything of them and from them. As you water a plant, the flowers are for the whole world. The beauty, the fragrance, the perfume, is for everyone who comes by. In the same way, are we willing to let the children grow in such a freedom, in such an atmosphere of trust, respect and affection that they we will be able to say and do things without any inhibitions whatsoever ?

When children are brought up in the atmosphere of affection and trust, in love and respect, they grow up without any inhibitions. They get the strength, they get the waters of your affection, they get the manure of your trust and faith in them and they then become strong enough to face any challenge of the world, any challenge of society. It is the inner strength that matters. It is the quality of fearlessness that matters. Not that we are going to equip them—if you are faced with this challenge, do this; if you are faced with that challenge, don't do that. Providing them with 'musts', 'must-nots', 'dos' and 'don'ts', providing them with norms and patterns, has been the way of bringing them up uptil now.

Now we have to wake up. Otherwise the gap between the parents and the children is going to go on widening. The gap between the teachers and the children is widening already. So, to bring back the harmony, the love and respect between the children and the parents, is absolutely necessary. I won't go into more details. Whatever I have said in relation to the first question is sufficient enough for the listeners to get an idea of the speaker's approach to such problems.

Question:--Where does one begin individually and collectively, in order to bring about a non-violent revolution without depending upon leaders ?

Answer:--Quite an exhaustive question. First of all, if I remember right, I have used the term total revolution and not non-violent revolution in my public talks. Perhaps the questioner has not attended the three talks given in this hall. The discussion meeting to-day is based really on the three talks given here on the total revolution where I had analysed in the first meeting the mechanism of mind, the functioniog, the operation of the cerebral organism, its dependence upon time and space, concepts, symbols. In the second, we proceeded to analyse the possibility, to explore the possibility of a non-cerebral and a non-mental discovery, transcending the frontiers of mind and brain in a non-cerebral, a non-mental way; and in the third, we proceeded to find out if it was necessary to look out for a Guru, a master, a teacher, before one launched upon this inner voyage, before one undertook this personal discovery of the meaning of life. So nowhere do I remember that I have used the phrase non-violent revolution, except in the students' meeting yesterday.

It was not a public meeting, a private meeting with the students where I was speaking to them what after Marx, Mao and Gandhi ? So this question is not bssed on the talks—and yet to respect the desire of the questioner, let us look at it. If one wants to bring about a non-violent revolution, if one wants to build a society based on non-violence, where does one begin individually and also collectively, without depending upon personality of leaders. Where are the individuals who have the very intense, very acute sense of self-respect and freedom that they will not like to depend upon a leader ? Politically, we want leaders. Economically, we want theoreticians, experts. In religion and culture, we want a master. Who wants freedom ?

Where are the individuals coming together, co-operating in mutual respect, working together in complete freedom without wanting a leader to conform to his behaviour, to accept his guidance, to feel secure under his leadership ? This immaturity, this juvenile approach of solving problems only under the protection of some authority, has to be eliminated from the human consciousness altogether. It will be a collective activity all the same. Efforts will have to be organised, individuals will have to come together but not under a leader. When they rally round a leader, they relegate all responsibility to the leader, they relax in their immaturity, following what he says, what he does.

If the Indians had not followed Mahatma Gandhi but if they had taken pains to understand what he meant by truth and non-violence, India would not be where she is to-day. It was not a collective activity. Individuals were following him, not understanding, appreciating. It was Gandhi's cause that hundreds of thousands were carrying out—it was not their own cause. And no revolution will take place unless mature individuals feel the urgency, the necessity, the gravity of the whole situation, the crisis in the human psyche as their own personal, individual concern. Unless there are individuals who feel that no revolution can take place because slaves cannot set others free. It is only a free individual vibrating with that sense of complete freedom who can impart that urge for freedom to others, So, first of all, Sir, the world needs a handful individuals who are willing to break new paths, not repeating the old slogans, not wanting to have security. They want to have a revolution, at the same time they want security. It can't be.

For those who are willing to expose themselves to the vulnerability, to the insecurity that a total change involves, it is no use talking about the 'how'. Now, let us suppose that there are handful individuals, I wonder if there are any. It was seventy-five years ago when a young Indian called Vivekananda wandered over the globe. He wandered all over India too. And you know what he said in 1898. He said.—"if I had half-a-dozen young men, the face of India would be changed." How many rallied round

that prince among human beings, Jesus of Nazreth, and among
those twelve one betrayed, and the other denied him thrice before
the night was over. We want to follow the leaders, Sir. So, when
you ask me how can individuals begin, individuals working collectively without depending upon the personality of leaders? I think
aloud and I say to myself—are there individuals who would like
to come together ? You may be having tiny lamps of your own
life, but instead of basking in any borrowed lights or other people's lights, it is glorious to carry the small earthen lamp of clay
in your own hand which may provide you light only for one or
two steps, willing to take those two steps, but in your own light.

Thus the first requirement of a revolution through love is
the individuals who are willing to become lights unto themselves
and who will not measure the success and failure of their revolutionary attempts and their theories and ideas in the scales of values of the bourgeois society. They will not weigh the success and
failure with money, with respectability. It is not important to
succeed. What is important is to bring a new light upon the human problems, to bring a new duality of consciousness, new quality
of perception, a new perspective to human problems. And if they
can do it, if they can stand in their own —what does it matter if
they commit mistakes ? But we are afraid of committing mistakes.

The first requirement is the individuals who are willing to
go through an inner transformation and grow into fearlessness, not
bravery. We have many brave people scattered round the globe.
But bravery is a counterpart of cowardice. Cowardice and bravery
are the obverse and the converse of the same inhibition of the
mind. Fearlessness is a qualitatively different state altogether. So,
handful individuals, growing into the maturity of fearlessness and
self-reliance, exploring the possibility of a total revolution are
needed. I would say, revolution through love, because the word
non-violence has been heavily loaded with many associations. It
has been pitched against violence. It has the implicit tension of
violence invisibly standing against it. Better not touch that word.
Let us use the word 'love'.

The dynamism of love has not been used as a motivation
force for socio-economic or political revolutions. It has been looked

upon as a religious thing, a spiritual value at best, useful for the saints, the monks, the Bhikshus, the Sanyasis, the Yogis, but not a value on which human relationships can be based. Economy based on co-operation, not on competition is needed. Administrations and political set-ups based upon the consent of people, and not on the sanction of violence are needed.

Nobody has looked upon dynamism of love as something which can be useful as a motivation force. Anger, jealousy, aggression, violence, conflict, competition, have been used as motivation forces for revolutions. Thousands of years man has used that, in the East as well as in the West. And the ruthlessness with which things are carried out under these motivation forces, has been confused with efficiency and competence. The illusion of speed that the ruthlessness creates, has been mistaken for the success of the revolutionary efforts.

Hence the challenge is to experiment with love and friendship, co-operation and respect, faith in the innate goodness of man. I call him a man of faith who has faith in the innate goodness of each human being. But even democracies are not based on this faith in the innate goodness of man, respect for the reason of human beings. So, we have to go a long way. Individuals will have to study the dynamism of love whether co-operation can replace competition, whether love can replace anger, hatred and jealousy, whether respect for man and faith in his innate goodness can replace jealousy, suspicion. All these will take us a step further—in the technique and method in the science and art of revolution. So, we will have to study these matters very seriously.

Individuals will have to begin by finding out. They will have to study the new dynamics of revolution, the new methods, the new techniques and they will have to find out if individually the roots of violence, aggression, and exploitation, are contained in their own psyche and to eliminate them simultaneously with the efforts to change the outer structures. It is no use saying that we eliminate the roots of violence from our psyche in isolation and then bring about socio-economic change. It is no use. It is no use saying on the other hand that we will change the socio-economic patterns first, then we will change the quality of consciousness. It has not happened.

The history of revolutions for the last fifty years, half a century. in different countries of the world is there. Let us learn from them, not condemn them, not deny them and search for a more decent, a more humane way. So where does the individual begin ? He, along-with his friends, if he has any, first studies. Human life is not to be lightly, casually, played with. One who has not studied, made a comparative study of the science and art, the techniques and methods and the dynamics of revolutions for the last half a century, will not be able to work in any country whatsoever.

Question:—In what way do Karma, rebirth and free will operate ?

Answer:—I do not remember to have used these words in any of my talks. If you start basing your talks on religious, cult·ural, philosophical or metaphysical terminology of any system, you are bound to enter into academic discussion. People belonging to various religions, respecting various metaphysical theories and philosophies, may be present here. These are questions based on the philosophy of Hinduism, the four pillars of Hindu religion. The law of immortality, the law of Karma, these two are implied in this question. But why should we enter into an academic disc·ussion ? Don't you think the speaker deserves a little co-operation in a discussion meeting and that co-operation can be expressed by making queries or comments upon what the speaker has said. otherwise, it will be spending the time of the gathering in specul-ative, theoretical or academic discussion.

Not that one can't go into the theory of Karma, the law of Karma, the law of causality, the law of causation, to express it in Western scientific terms. Then you have to refer to 'Prarabdha,' 'Sanchita,' 'Kriyamana.' These are the three differentiations of Karma. You have to refer to the theory of immortality of the soul. So, what is Atman ? What is the soul and what is mortality and immortality ? You will have to enter into all those metaphysical discussions. And why does not man limit first his perceptions to his own life, between the points of birth and death ? We will have to live here on this earth, like mature human beings in sanity, in love, in friendship. We have not been able to do that. We have had thousands of books in the East and the West about the theories how the world was created, whether the God is personal or impersonal, whether there is 'dvaita' or 'advaita', whether there is rebirth or not, agnosticism, atheism etc. There are Saddarshanas, six systems of philosophy, as far as the Hindus are concerned.

What are we going to do by entering into discussions based on theories arrived at by other people ? If I say, when the body dies, there is an element of consciousness which does not die, how does that help ? Do we know what death is ? Do we know what dying is ? We are not conscious even of what we are doing in the waking hours. Even to-day from morning uptil now we have been just floating passively on the ways and patterns of behaviour without doing them in a mindful state. We have been reacting according to the patterns and ways of behaviour. We don't know, we have not been aware. Birth is not an experience for us, nor is death. Living is not a first hand experience and event for us, nor is dying; and we would like to talk about rebirth. What use will it be if I say that life never dies, death is an illusion ? The body does not die. It changes the form. So out of the five elements, the element of fire becomes one with the element of fire in the universe, and the element of water gets mingled in the universal water and so on. If I go on describing how the five elements get merged into the five elements existing outside the skin, how does it help ? How does it help to change the quality of my relationship with you ?

I will go home and get angry with you all the same, annoyed with you all the same. Talk of the law of Karma, rebirth, immortality and I will be afraid and scared of death, all the same. Intellectual acquisition of an idea is not understanding of fact. This intellectual acquisition of ideas and theories, making small changes here and great changes there, doing patch-work with ways of behaviour—doesn't change the quality of your and my life; and the crisis is too grave. We have to change the texture, the quality of our relationships here and now.

"The freedom of will"—Is there free will ? Is there destiny ?

Does that destiny rule our lives or are we free ? Do we know what will is ? We do not know what desire is. You know we have wishes, the desire, the urge, the passion. We have not got the intensity even to feel a desire which will become a flame, and set the whole person ablaze, which won't allow him to rest until that desire is quenched.

Destiny is the cumulative effect of varions currents set in motion by individuals and groups of individuals, races and countries and religious entities. The currents invisible—psychological currents, the psychic currents set in motion from the very first human being who must have inhabited the globe, are functioning, they are operating. And whatever one does, one is surrounded by these currents. There are ways of making these currents co-operate with you, of merging yourself into those currents. There is a science of getting acquainted with these invisible currents, which are existing, which are operating. The cumulative effect of those currents at any given time in life is called fate, is called destiny. There are ways and ways of getting acquainted with their nature, with their trends, and educating the human beings, so that there is no conflict, but there is a harmony between these universal currents and the human relationships.

But I don't think these theoretical discussions have any practical value because I have come across thousands of temples, Maths, monasteries, churches, mosques, where people read such books, go on conducting discussions; and they are surrounded by illiterate people, people in ill-health, people starving around them; and inside the four walls the discnssions about the theory of Karma are going on. The pathos, the tragedy of it ! So I hope to be forgiven if I do not enter into an academic or theoretical discussion.

Question:—Do we need concepts of God and Divinity ?

Answer:—Can we have concept of air, water, earth, the skies ? You are living in them. I remember about six years ago a friend from the United States had come to Mount Abu, a small town where I live in India. That was his first visit to India. He wanted to meet the illiterate farmers, the villagers, the unsophisticated folk. So I was taking him around. In one of the villages we stopped the jeep, he got down. He wanted to talk to an old farmer and he was asking him do you believe in God ? I was to translate the questions and the answers both. So the first question my friend asked was—do you believe in God ? The farmer was astounded beyond words. He pointed to the Sun in the sky and he said to my friend do you believe in the Sun ?

The Doctor thought that the illiterate fellow had not understood his question. So he asked another question. He said, there is matter and there is spirit, do you believe in spirit, that is God, not the matter ? He pointed to the earth saying, 'not this dead matter. Do you believe in God, the spirit ?' You will be surprised the farmer took a handful of earth, kissed it and he said, do you dare call this dead, this mother earth which gives you grains, the scents of the flowers, the juices of fruits and vegetables ? You call my mother earth dead, and there were tears in his eyes. The Doctor, my sociologist friend, had no more questions to ask.

Sir, why do you need the concept of God and Divinity—personal or impersonal ? Personal and impersonal, tangible and intangible, visible and invisible, these are the reflections on the limitations of our sense-organs. not on the quality of existence by which we are surrounded. Obviously, we live in the ocean of energy, Sir, surrounded by the vibrations of energy, clothed in different shells and crusts. Some have thin crusts and some have thick ones. Even what you call matter is the most immaterial thing now-a-days, because matter is the abode of the energy. So what is my concept of God ? Is God personal or impersonal ? He defies your distinctions of personality and impersonality. He defies your distinctions of theisms and atheisms, beliefs and disbeliefs, your beliefs and your doubts. It is the totality of existence. Don't you see the life in the rays of light ?

In the day time have you ever looked at the rays of the Sun vibrating with life ? Have you ever observed the glowing colours of an evening sky ? Those colours are not dead. So, one has to intensify the sensitivity, not rely upon these defective sense-organs. No sense-organ of a human being can come into contact with the totality of any given objet. When I see this microphone standing here, do I see the whole of it ? Are my eyes capable of perceiving the totality of any unit of perception at any given moment in time ? So, one wonders if the sense organs can receive the impression of the totality of the object, whether the sensation released by those impressions inside the body are carried totally by the nervous system to the brain and whether the totality of those impulses and sensations are intetpreted by the conditioned brain. You see the limitations through which human beings have to work.

So as long as we perceive through the sense-organs, as long as we react through the brain, we will see life divided into personality and impersonality, tangibility and intangibility, the known and the unknown. But there is a way of perceiving non-cerebrally. There is a way of direct and immediate contact with reality. Perception born of non-duality and response born of spontaneity, that is to live in God, that is to live in the awareness of life. The element of earth contained in your body—does it belong to George, or Harry or Mary or Vimala or Kamala ? The element of water, the element of fire contained in the body—do they belong to the individual ? As long as this myth of the 'I' consciousness, the myth of perceiving and reacting only through the sense organs and only through the brain are left like that, as long as that myth is not exploded, as long as we are victims of that myth, God will be a concept and a theory.

Sir, do not let God be a concept and theory to be imprisoned in the pages of the books and the images and idols in the temples and the churches. Let him become the reality of life. He is the substance. The invisible, the unmanifest is the substance, the visible and the known is only the shadow. This is the conceptualisation and ideation of the reality that has made man fight. Have you not read history ? My God, your God—and wars being fought in the name of gods, the concepts and theories about divinity ! The Catholics and Protesants—have not you seen how they have been fighting in Ireland ? Hindus and Muslims fighting in India, Pakistan : the Arabs and the Isrealies, Jews fighting in the Middle East. Those who have done away with the concepts and theories of God and Divinity have installed State and political theories in place of the religious scriptures. They worship their States. They worship their political theories—and wars are waged in the names of ideologies, States and countries.

As long as God or Divinity remains on the conceptual and ideational level we are going to use those concepts and theories as weapons for our ego-centric activities, for our desire for power. Then the Bible will be used as a weapon and the books by Marx and Mao will be used as weapons. Then the Geeta will be used against Quran. It is being used. So, whether you take away the concept of God and instal State in place of God, whether you turn away from the churches and temples and instal all the sanctity in the buraucracy in place of religious priests, the preachers and teachers, the misery, sorrow will be the same.

I do feel no individual should live according to concepts, theories and ideas. Let him try to understand life first hand and live on the foundation cf that understanding. The content of understanding is the only richness and glory of individual's life. Not what I approximate my life to, not what I conform to, not what I follow, ape and imitate—that's all second-hand and we are second-hand human beings. Let us become first-hand human beings. Take the trouble of looking at life squarely in face as it comes, understand the challenges as they come and face them in our humble ways. All of us cannot become Buddhas and Jesuses and Gandhis. But a tiny little lamp burning with that tender flame is infinitely more important and significant than a rich borrowed light which you can neither light up, nor can you extinguish.

Hence let us drop this game of borrowing, imposing, accepting, conforming and following. Let us begin afresh in educational institutions, at homes, emphasising this personal understanding and discovery of truth. You know when you slightly change the emphasis in the ascent of a melody or in the descent, it changes the whole complexion. The quality, the character of the melody is changed by slightly changing the emphasis. Changing the interval between two notes, you change the whole music. In the some way, if you want to change the disharmony, the bitterness, the violence, that is to say, the disturbed melody of universal life, if you want to put it right, the key to be pressed is the individual life. Begin with oneself not by turning away, but being there as one is.

The time is over and so are the questions. To-morrow morning I leave Colombo for going north and I offer my sincere thanks and gratefulness to each one of you who has come here and given me such rapt attention.

•